Enid Blyton

THE
SECRET
SEVEN
COLLECTION 4

Have you read them all?

1 The Secret Seven
2 Secret Seven Adventure
3 Well Done, Secret Seven
4 Secret Seven on the Trail
5 Go Ahead, Secret Seven
6 Good Work, Secret Seven
7 Secret Seven Win Through
8 Three Cheers, Secret Seven
9 Secret Seven Mystery
10 Puzzle for the Secret Seven
11 Secret Seven Fireworks
12 Good Old Secret Seven
13 Shock for the Secret Seven
14 Look Out, Secret Seven
15 Fun for the Secret Seven

THE
SECRET
SEVEN

COLLECTION 4

PUZZLE FOR THE SECRET SEVEN

SECRET SEVEN FIREWORKS

GOOD OLD SECRET SEVEN

Illustrated by
Burgess Sharrocks

Hodder
Children's
Books

HODDER CHILDREN'S BOOKS

Puzzle for the Secret Seven first published in Great Britain in 1958
by Hodder and Stoughton
Secret Seven Fireworks first published in Great Britain in 1959
by Hodder and Stoughton
Good Old Secret Seven first published in Great Britain in 1960
by Hodder and Stoughton
This edition published 2017

1 3 5 7 9 10 8 6 4 2

A CIP catalogue record for this book is available from the British Library.

ISBN 978 1 444 93484 7

Typeset in Times by Avon DataSet Ltd, Bidford-on-Avon, Warwickshire

Printed and bound in Great Britain by Clays Ltd, St Ives plc

The paper and board used in this book are made from wood from responsible sources

Hodder Children's Books
An imprint of Hachette Children's Group
Part of Hodder and Stoughton
Carmelite House
50 Victoria Embankment
London EC4Y 0DZ

An Hachette UK Company
www.hachette.co.uk
www.hachettechildrens.co.uk

PUZZLE FOR THE SECRET SEVEN

Contents

1 Off to the fair 1
2 A good time – and a shock! 8
3 The fire at Hilly-Down 15
4 Secret Seven meeting 22
5 All kinds of plans! 29
6 An afternoon of hard work! 36
7 Susie and Binkie are a nuisance 43
8 Matt has surprising news 50
9 Crash! 57
10 Very surprising 61
11 A very interesting meeting 71
12 Scamper makes a find 77
13 An odd little boy 84
14 Something very strange 90
15 Up on the hills at night 97
16 The strange wailing 103
17 Where is the violin? 110
18 An unexpected find 117
19 Little Benny 124
20 Meeting of the Secret Nine! 132

CHAPTER ONE

Off to the fair

'HALLO!' SHOUTED a voice over the wall, and Scamper barked loudly at once. Peter and Janet looked up from their gardening.

'Oh, hallo, Jack!' said Peter, pleased. 'Stop barking, Scamper! Anyone would think you hadn't seen Jack for a month. Come on in, Jack. Any news?'

'Yes. Rather nice news,' said Jack, wheeling his bicycle in at the front gate. 'My mother won ten pounds at the whist drive last night – and she's given it to me to take all the Secret Seven over to the fair at Hilly-Down today. Can you and Janet come?'

'That's very decent of your mother,' said Peter, and Janet beamed. She had so badly wanted to go to the fair, but she and Peter were saving up for their father's birthday.

'There's just one thing, though,' said Jack, seriously. 'Susie will have to come too – and she's got an awful friend staying with her, called Binkie. Mother says the money's for them too.'

'Oh well – we can put up with Susie for once in a way,' said Peter. 'After all, it's not as if we were going out to solve some mystery, or are in the middle of an adventure. You tell your mother we're very, very grateful. What time shall we meet?'

'Let's go after tea, when there are crowds of people at the fair,' said Jack. 'And stay till the lights are on. I love those great flaring lights they have. Let's meet at about five o'clock at the bus-stop in the High Street. And don't pay any attention to Susie and Binkie if they giggle all the time!'

'We certainly won't,' said Peter. 'Righto, then – meet you at five o'clock. Are all the others coming?'

'Yes. I've been round to them,' said Jack, getting on his bicycle. 'We'll have at least a pound each to spend, and some of the others are bringing a bit more too. See you at five, then!'

He rode off, ringing his bell in farewell. Peter and Janet were pleased. 'We'd better ask Mother,' said Janet. 'Though I'm sure she'll say we can go – especially as we've promised to garden all day!'

Mother said of course they could go, and she would add three pounds to the money Jack's mother had given. Scamper listened to it all, wagging his tail. He looked up at Peter and gave a little whine.

'He wants to know if he can go too,' said Peter, with a laugh. 'Yes, if you can keep up with our bikes, Scamper, old thing. You're getting a bit fat, you know!'

Scamper barked joyfully. There was nothing he liked better than an outing with the Secret Seven.

'You haven't had many meetings lately, down in your shed,' said Mother. 'Has the Secret Seven broken up?'

'Oh *no*, Mother!' said Peter and Janet together, quite shocked. Mother laughed.

'Well, a week of your Easter holidays has already gone, and you haven't asked me for cakes and lemonade for one of your mysterious meetings yet,' she said. 'And I bought quite a big tin of biscuits, thinking I'd have to supply you Seven with something to nibble at your meetings!'

'Nothing's happened yet for us to call a meeting about,' said Janet. 'But we've still got two weeks' holiday left.'

'Woof!' said Scamper, agreeing heartily, and wagging his tail.

'Your life is *all* holiday, Scamper!' said Peter. 'You don't do a single stroke of work – and it's no good your trying to tell me that you helped us with the digging this morning! All *you* were doing was digging up a bone you'd hidden!'

At five o'clock quite a crowd of children arrived on bicycles at the bus-stop in the High Street. First came Peter and Janet, punctual as usual, because Peter said that as leader he must always be on time. Just after came Colin, out of breath with racing along fast in case he was late. Then came Pam and Barbara together, with George shouting behind.

'Six of us,' said Janet. 'We just want Jack and Susie and Binkie. What a name! We once had a rabbit called Binkie, do you remember, Peter? It had a dear little twitchy nose, and teeth that stuck out.'

'Here they are,' said George, as three children came cycling quickly round the corner. 'Hallo, Jack!'

'Sorry we're last,' said Jack. 'But you know what Susie is – couldn't find her purse, didn't know where her bike was . . .'

'Oooh, you fibber,' said Susie. 'You know you kept us waiting while you pumped up your front tyre. Binkie, this is the rest of the wonderful Secret Seven that I told you Jack belonged to.'

Binkie beamed all round, and Janet nudged Peter in delight. 'She's like our rabbit!' she said, in a low voice. 'Exactly!'

Peter wanted to laugh, because Janet was right. Binkie had a funny little twitchy nose, and teeth just like a rabbit. She only needed

nice long furry ears. She was a terrible chatterbox, even worse than Susie.

'Oh, hello!' she said, in a breathless voice. 'It's so nice to meet you all. Susie's told me all about you. And is this Scamper? Oh my, isn't he lovely? I've got a dog at home too, but he's a terrier, and you should see him catch a . . .'

'Shut up, Binkie,' said Jack, firmly. 'And please don't wobble on your bike when you ride with us. I never *saw* such a wobbler before!'

'Oh well, you see, it's because I always . . .' began Binkie, but nobody listened. They all

6

rode off, chattering and laughing, Scamper running delightedly with them.

The fair was about a mile and a half away at Hilly-Down. It was in a big field, and as the children topped the last hill and looked down on the colourful sight they were full of delight.

'All those tents and stalls, and flags flying and fluttering!' said Jack, as he cycled down the hill.

'And the roundabout! I can hear its music quite clearly,' said Janet. 'Oooh, Binkie, don't wobble so – you nearly had me off.'

They came to the entrance of the field, and went in. They stacked their bicycles carefully together in a corner, and Peter called to Scamper.

'On guard, Scamper!' he said, pointing to the nine bicycles. 'On guard, old boy!'

Scamper badly wanted to go with them, but he felt proud to be on guard. He wagged his tail and lay down by the bicycles. Peter patted him, and turned to the others.

'Now come on,' he said. 'Into the fair we go!'

CHAPTER TWO

A good time – and a shock!

THE FAIR was very good indeed. The round-about especially was voted 'brilliant' by everyone.

'It's the *quickest* roundabout I ever knew,' said George, when they were all getting off after a very dizzy ride. 'I had to cling on to my giraffe for dear life. I was nearly swung off! Have we enough money to go again?'

'I don't want to go on again,' said Pam, trying to walk straight. 'I still feel as if I'm going round and round on my lion. Oooh, sorry, Colin – I didn't mean to bump into you. I just can't walk properly!'

Binkie was the same, and everyone laughed at the two girls, they were so dizzy. 'Let's go to the hoopla stall,' said Jack. 'But we won't let

Pam or Binkie have throws, because they'll be too giddy to aim properly.'

That made both Pam and Binkie much more sensible, of course. In fact, Pam recovered so quickly that she threw best of the lot, and managed to get a hoop round a box of sweets, which she promptly shared with the others.

There was a coconut shy over in one corner, and here Peter shone, because he was an excellent thrower. He knocked down three coconuts, and the man in charge of the shy wasn't at all pleased! He handed Peter the coconuts with a very bad grace.

'However do you do it, Peter?' asked Jack, enviously. 'You *always* get a coconut when you go to a fair. And today you've got three!'

'Well, I pretend I'm bowling at a wicket,' said Peter, 'and the coconut I aim at is the row of stumps! It's easy if you think of it like that!'

Everyone immediately wanted to have another throw, but George shook his head. 'No. There's not enough money,' he said. 'Not even with Peter's extra money – unless you don't want to try anything else.'

But they all wanted to go on the big wheel, so, much to the coconut-shy man's relief, they moved off. 'Let's put these coconuts beside our bikes,' said Peter. 'I don't want to carry them about all the time. Scamper will guard them.'

Scamper was delighted to see them. He was lying by the pile of bicycles keeping an eye on everyone who passed. If anyone came a little nearer the bicycles than he thought they ought to, he stood up at once and growled. Two other dogs sat near by, admiring Scamper's fierceness. He was really feeling rather important.

Peter threw the coconuts down beside the bicycles. 'On guard, Scamper,' he said, and Scamper gave a short, sharp bark, as if to say, 'Yes, sir, certainly, sir!' He ran to the coconuts, sniffed them all over, then lay down again, keeping a sharp eye on the other two dogs.

The nine children spent every penny of their money, and then wished they had a little left to spend on some delicious-smelling hot ginger-bread. This was being made in a little oven by a small, fat, gipsy-looking woman. It looked good and smelt even better.

'Want to buy some?' she asked Peter.

'Yes – but we haven't any money left,' said Peter. She laughed, and pushed a small batch of rather crumbly gingerbread squares over to them.

'Help yourselves. These are done a bit too much. I can't sell them.'

'Thanks! That's nice of you,' said Peter, and he and the others helped themselves. He saw a pram nearby, with a baby laughing in it. It was rather a dirty baby, and the pram was old, broken-down and dirty too – but the baby was such a merry little creature that no one could help watching it as they munched the delicious gingerbread.

Janet went to play with the baby, and it held out its hands, and bounced up and down in delight. 'Does the baby travel about with the fair?' Janet asked the mother.

'Oh, no. We live up in a shack on the hillside,' said the little fat woman. 'My husband goes round with the fair when it wants extra help, and when it comes anywhere in the district I sell gingerbread.' She saw some people coming up, and began to shout. 'Hot gingerbread, real old-fashioned gingerbread, straight from the oven. Twenty pence a piece, only twenty pence a piece!'

'Come on,' said Peter, looking at his watch. 'We really ought to go now. We'll just wander once more round the fair now all the lights are up.'

'I like it better when it gets dark and they light those big flares,' said Janet. 'This is just the time I love. What a pity we've got to go!'

'I think I'll stay on a bit longer with Binkie,' said Susie. 'You like the fair when it's night-time, don't you, Binkie?'

'Oh, *yes*,' gushed Binkie, her nose twitching. 'It's so – so sort of romantic. It makes me want to write poetry. Oh, do let's stay, Susie. The others can go if they want to. I might be able to write a poem about it.'

'Binkie writes marvellous poetry,' announced Susie proudly. 'She won a prize at school for it. You ought to hear her recite it.'

This was the very last thing that anyone wanted. They stared at Binkie in horror, for it was plain that she was quite prepared to recite to them then and there.

'I said it was *time to go*,' said Peter, in a very determined voice. 'And you and Binkie are to come too, Susie. We can't leave you here alone.'

'Oh yes you can. *I* don't belong to your silly Secret Seven,' said Susie at once. '*I'm* not under your orders.'

'Well, you're under *mine*,' said Jack firmly. 'And you know that Mother said you were to come back with *me*. And we are going RIGHT NOW!'

Susie said no more, but she scowled. 'She'll pay us back for this,' said Jack to Peter. 'Good thing we haven't a meeting coming on – she and Binkie would try to spoil it! Come *on*, Susie!'

They collected their bicycles from a delighted Scamper, and set off back home again. But on the way up the hill that led from the fair, George spied something that astonished him – a great light on the hillside, not far to the left.

'What's that?' he shouted, and stopped for the others to catch him up. 'Look – flames – and smoke! It's a house on fire!'

'Goodness, yes – we'd better see if we can help!' said Peter. 'Look, there's a telephone box just there, on the other side of the road, George. I'll telephone the fire brigade, while you others cut across the field-path there, and see what's happening. Hurry up!'

He rode to the telephone box and went inside, while the others opened the field gate and then rode at top speed up the narrow path that led to the fire. *Was* it a house burning fiercely – it didn't look as if much could be saved!

In the telephone box Peter asked for the fire brigade, and spoke urgently into the telephone mouthpiece. 'Hallo! Fire brigade? There's a fire up here on Hilly-Down Hill. It looks pretty fierce. Right – we'll stay here till you come!'

CHAPTER THREE

The fire at Hilly-Down

PETER LET the telephone box door swing shut, jumped on his bicycle, and cycled along the same path as the others. He caught them up as he came to the fire, and stared in horror. Whatever had stood there on the hillside was almost burnt out!

'What was it? A house?' he asked, shielding his eyes from the fierceness of the roaring flames. 'I hope no one was in it!'

'A ginger cat was the only live thing we saw,' said George, looking very solemn. 'It shot by us as we came up. It must have been a small house, Peter. Did you get on to the fire brigade?'

'Yes. They're coming. But it will be too late,' said Peter. 'Janet, don't cry. I don't expect there was anyone in the place.'

'Well – it must have been old and rotten to go up as quickly as that,' said Colin. 'What a crackling and roaring! Look out, Barbara – there are bits of burning stuff blowing about still.'

Peter took Jack with him, and the two boys anxiously walked all round the burning house, trying to see if there was anything they could do. But there was nothing to be seen but flames, now dying down a little, and tumbled, smoking pieces of wood. No wonder the poor old cat had been terrified!

Then came the sound of a loud siren, and Colin called out in excitement. 'The fire-engine! Hasn't it been quick? Well, they can't help seeing at once where the fire is!'

'We left the field gate open, didn't we?' said George, and Peter nodded. 'Yes – and look, the fire-engine's coming through it now. Gosh, I wish *I* could drive it!'

The fire-engine came slowly up the narrow, rutted path, gleaming brightly in the light from the roaring fire. 'Anyone know if there's a well?' shouted a fireman, leaping down to unroll a long hose-pipe.

'There's a stream running down the hill just

here!' called Jack, and the firemen went over to it. In less than a minute they were playing water on the flames, and a great sizzling noise arose.

'Like a million bacon rashers frying at once,' said Janet in wonder, and she was right!

'Did you see anyone about?' asked one of the firemen, as the flames died down under the water.

'No. Nobody,' said Peter. 'But the whole place was on fire when we came up – nobody could have been saved if anyone *had* been in there. But surely they would have run out, wouldn't they?'

'Might have been children asleep there,' said the man shortly. 'Whose is this shack?'

Nobody knew – but just then Peter saw someone hurrying up the field-path, wheeling something in front of her that bumped wildly over the ruts.

'It's the woman who was making ginger-bread at the fair!' cried Janet. 'Oh – she said she lived in a shack on the hill-top. It must be *her* place! Poor, poor thing!'

It *was* the gingerbread woman. She came up quite breathless, her eyes staring in fright, the baby being almost bumped out of its pram.

'My Benny!' she shouted. 'Where is he? I left him here.'

'Well, Mam – we haven't *seen* anyone about,' said the chief fireman, and a little shiver of horror went through the children. No! No, surely no one could have been in that burning shack!

'Benny, Benny, Benny! Where are you, my little Benny?' screamed the woman. And then, to everyone's enormous relief, a child's high voice answered shakily from somewhere.

'Mammy! Mammy! Mammy!'

'He's safe,' said the little gingerbread woman, and tears ran down her cheeks. 'I'll go find him. He won't come out while everyone's staring round. He's in the bushes somewhere, my little Benny.'

She took the baby out of its pram, and carrying him in her arms, she hurried in the direction of a row of thick bushes a little way below the still-burning shack. 'Benny!' she called. 'Benny! Mammy's here. Everything's all right, love.'

And then, quite suddenly, it seemed as if there was a whole crowd of people staring at the dying fire – people who had left the fair, seen the flames, and come hurrying in at the open gate. Perhaps the woman's husband was there too? The children hoped so. Then he could comfort the poor little woman.

'What will they do for the night?' wondered Janet. 'Where will they sleep?'

'Oh, someone will lend them a barn, or take them in for the night,' said one of the firemen, busy rolling up the hose. 'It's a mercy no one was hurt. You kids go along home now. Thanks for letting us know.'

'I wish we'd some money left,' said Jack, thinking that the money his mother had given him would have been a godsend to the gingerbread woman just now.

Two policemen arrived, and one began taking notes. The other moved the crowd away. 'Move along, please,' he said. 'The fire's over. We can't do anything more. Will you move along, sir, please? And you too, madam?'

He came to the little crowd of children, still standing there with Scamper, feeling rather miserable.

'Are you the kids who warned the fire brigade?' he said. 'Well, that was good work on your part. But get along home now, please. You can't do anything more.'

'What will happen to the poor woman and her children now?' asked Peter. 'I mean – she must have lost everything in the fire.'

'We'll look after her and the family,' said the policeman, stolidly. 'She'll be all right. That was only an old shack they lived in, not a house – they didn't have much of anything. You go home now, please, and let us do what we can for the woman.'

The fire-engine departed with its siren blaring, trying to make the crowd get out of its way. The children found their bicycles and wheeled them to the gate, Scamper following, wondering if they were going home. What an evening!

They all mounted their bicycles and rode along the road, very silent. Even Susie found nothing to say. Binkie began to talk first, the words suddenly pouring out.

'I've never seen a fire before, I've

never seen a fire-engine so close. Ooh, wasn't it exciting? I've never . . .'

'Be quiet,' said Peter. 'You make it sound as if it was a sort of treat! Think of that poor woman!'

'Yes. *I'm* thinking about her too,' said George. 'I say, Peter – I think we ought to call a meeting of the Secret Seven, and see if we can't plan something to help her. What about tomorrow morning at ten o'clock?'

'Fine idea!' said Peter, really pleased. 'I was just thinking the same thing myself. Secret Seven, those are your orders – be down in our shed, ten o'clock tomorrow morning.'

'Susie and me too?' said Binkie, thrilled.

'No,' said Peter. 'ONLY the Secret Seven. Susie – do you hear that? ONLY the Secret Seven!'

CHAPTER FOUR

Secret Seven meeting

NEXT MORNING, sharp at five to ten, Peter and
Janet were down in their shed. On the door
were the letters S.S., and everything was ready
inside – boxes to sit on, some biscuits on a
plate, and lemonade to drink.

'I hope everyone remembers the password,
and their badges,' said Peter. 'It's rather a long
time since we had the last meeting.'

'Wuff!' said Scamper, suddenly wagging his
tail. Janet gave a squeal of laughter.

'*Scamper* knows it! He said it! Yes, Scamper,
you've remembered the password – it was
Wuff! Clever dog!'

Footsteps came up the path to the shed, and
Scamper gave a little whine of welcome. He
knew it was George. A knock came on the door,

and a low voice said, 'Wuff!'

'Enter!' called Peter, and George came in, grinning, wearing his badge on his coat.

'I nearly forgot the password,' he said. 'But luckily I'd written it down in my diary! Here comes someone else.'

It was Pam and Barbara. They knocked, and Peter called out immediately, 'Password, please.'

'Peter, we're not quite sure if it's Wuff or Woof,' said Pam's anxious voice.

'Wuff!' said Scamper at once.

'You're *not* to give the password away, Scamper,' said Janet, shocked. Barbara and Pam giggled outside the door. 'Thanks, Scamper. Wuff, Peter!'

'Come in,' said Peter. 'Just by the skin of your teeth, though! Who's that coming now?'

'Jack and Colin,' said Pam, as the door shut on her and Barbara. 'Oh, it's good to be here again, in our shed!'

Knock-knock!

'Password!' called Peter. 'And DON'T yell it.'

'We've forgotten it,' said Colin, in a very apologetic voice. 'I mean – it's so long since we had a meeting, and . . .'

'Can't let you in!' said Peter sternly.

'Oh, don't be such an idiot, Peter,' said Jack angrily. 'You know I daren't write our password down in case Susie finds it – and it's awfully difficult to remember it when we have had so many. I know it's something to do with a dog. Is it Whiskers?'

'Wuff, wuff, wuff,' said Scamper, and Pam gave a squeal of delight. Then a voice came from somewhere in the bushes outside.

'The password is Wuff, Jack, Wuff!' and then came a burst of very loud laughter from two people.

'SUSIE! BINKIE! I TOLD you not to follow me!' cried Jack angrily. 'How do *you* know the password?'

'Oh, come in, come in,' said Peter, opening the door. Jack and Colin went in, looking angry, and Peter went over to the bushes. He spoke sternly to the two giggling girls behind them.

'Spoil-sports! Go and giggle somewhere else. If you are here in two minutes' time I shall take the hose-pipe and water this bush thoroughly. And I *mean* that!'

There was a scuffling noise, and the two girls ran off, still giggling. Susie knew that Peter meant what he said, and she didn't want to be hosed! Peter went into the shed and slammed the door.

To everyone's great relief, he said nothing at all about passwords. 'Now,' he said, taking his place on his box. 'About this business of the fire. I've . . .'

But before he could go on, Scamper began to bark madly. He ran to the door and scraped at it, still barking.

'Scamper! What's all this row about?' demanded Peter. 'If it's those two girls again you're to go and chase them away. Do you hear?'

Scamper was delighted to see Peter opening the door. He dashed out at once, and the Secret Seven looked after him to see if he was chasing Susie and Binkie.

But he wasn't. He was dancing round two legs in corduroy trousers, his tail wagging in delight.

'Oh, it's Dad's shepherd,' said Peter, in surprise, and called to the fine-looking old man on the nearby path. 'Hallo, Matt! Did you want my father? He's gone to market, I'm afraid.'

'Oh. I was afraid he'd be gone,' said old Matt, taking his cap off and scratching his thatch of grey hair. 'Well – maybe you'd give him a message for me, Peter?'

'Yes, of course,' said Peter. 'What is it?'

'Well, you probably know there was a fire last night over on Hilly-Down,' said Matt, 'and

Luke Bolan and his wife had their shack burnt out, and they've nowhere to go . . .'

'Yes – we all saw it,' said Peter soberly. 'And I telephoned for the fire brigade, Matt.'

'You did? That was smart of you, Peter,' said Matt. 'Well, now, I've got an idea to put to your father – but you say he's at the market?'

'Yes. He won't be home till after dinner,' said Peter. 'What's your idea, Matt?'

'There's an old caravan up by my sheep-hut,' said Matt. 'I lived in it before your father built me my hut, and I only use it now to store my goods in. Proper broken-down old thing it is – but it would house Luke Bolan and his wife and kids for a bit, Peter, if your father would let him use it. They haven't anywhere to go, you see?'

'Oh, I'm *sure* my father would let them have it,' said Peter, and Janet nodded at once. 'Anyway, let's go and ask Mother. She'll know if Dad would give permission.'

So the whole of the Secret Seven, with old Matt and Scamper too, went up the garden-path and round the house to where Peter's mother was weeding her lettuce bed. She was most surprised to see them with the shepherd.

'Why, Matt!' she said. 'Is anything the matter?'

Matt told her what he had said to Peter, and she listened carefully. 'Of course the Bolans can have the caravan until they can find somewhere else,' she said. 'I know my husband would say that. That poor woman – all her things burnt up like that. We'll certainly have to do something to help her. You go back to the Bolans, Matt, and tell them they can move into the old caravan at once. You can take your things out and store them in your own hut for a time, can't you?'

'Oh yes,' said Matt. 'And I can give them a rug, and lend them my little old table.'

'We'll see what we can do too,' said Peter's mother, and she turned to the Secret Seven. 'Will you let me come to your meeting for once?' she said. 'Because I think we can all help in this – and if I'm there I can help you to make sensible plans. It's a thing we must do together.'

'Of course, Mother!' said Peter, delighted. 'Come along now, this very minute! We'd LOVE to have you!'

CHAPTER FIVE

All kinds of plans!

THE SECRET Seven filed into the shed after Peter and Janet's mother. Peter shut the door.

'I'm glad you didn't ask me for the password, Peter,' said his mother, smiling. 'Dear me, I do feel important, coming to one of your meetings. It's very nice of you to let me.'

'We're very pleased, Mother,' said Janet, and all the others nodded in agreement. Everyone liked Peter and Janet's kind, generous mother.

They began to talk about the fire, and the homeless Bolans.

'There's Luke Bolan, Mother, who goes round with the fair,' said Peter, 'and there's Mrs Bolan, who visits any fair that comes into the district, and makes hot gingerbread to sell.

We hadn't any money left to buy it, but she gave us all some!'

'That was really very kind of her,' said his mother surprised.

'And there's a dear, smiley little baby,' said Pam. 'Rather dirty, but a darling.'

'And there's a boy called Benny,' said Janet. 'We haven't actually seen him, Mother. He was in the shack last night when it was burnt down, but he ran out and hid in the bushes. Poor Mrs Bolan was so afraid he would be inside the burning shack.'

'Yes. You told me last night,' said her mother. 'Well, now, let's think. I suggest that each of you should go home and tell your mothers about what has happened – and tell them that we are going to lend the old caravan to the Bolans, but that as all their things were burnt, we want to try and give them as many really necessary things as we can . . .'

'Do you mean kettles and things?' asked Pam.

'Yes – and perhaps an old mattress to sleep on,' said Peter's mother. 'There won't be room for a bed, of course. A folding chair would be a good idea – and a small mattress perhaps for the little boy and the baby. They will want food too.'

'Well, I'm really glad that the Secret Seven have something to do,' said Peter, pleased. 'It makes us much more of a real club then. What can *you* give, Mother?'

'There's an old mattress in the loft,' said his mother, thinking hard. 'And I can send up at least one saucepan – and I've an old blanket, and . . .'

'Well, if all our mothers can find something or other we'll be able to make that caravan really cosy,' said Janet, looking forward to the job. 'I vote that everyone goes home after this meeting, and finds out what he or she can bring – and then comes back here to another meeting as soon after dinner as possible . . .'

'And we'll draw up a list of things, and choose what we think Mrs Bolan will need!' said Peter. 'Mother can help in that, can't you, Mother?'

'Oh yes!' said his mother, smiling. 'And when we've decided what to take we'll get the farm-van, and pile everything into it. We'd better take a scrubbing-brush or two, because I expect that old caravan will need cleaning.'

'This *is* going to be fun,' said Barbara. 'I'm good at cleaning! I only hope Mrs Bolan won't be there, because it would be wonderful to see her face when she comes to the van, and sees it all clean and furnished ready for her!'

'Oooh yes – I'd like to get it all quite perfect,' said Pam. 'Shall we go off home now?'

'Yes,' said Peter. 'The sooner the better! Now mind you tell your mothers what *my* mother has said – and I bet they'll all rush round and see what they can find.'

The Seven stood up, excited, and Scamper wagged his tail eagerly, jumping up at Peter. 'Do you want to help too, old fellow?' said Peter. 'Well, we'll take you with us! Now remember, Secret Seven – back here after dinner

– say as near half-past two as possible. And
REMEMBER THE PASSWORD!'

'Wuff!' said the rest of the Seven at once,
and made Scamper bark in delight.

'Thank you, Mother, for coming to our
meeting,' said Janet, hugging her mother. 'We'll
bring you our lists this afternoon and let you
say which things would be best to take up to the
old caravan. Won't Matt be surprised to see
us?'

'He certainly will,' said her mother. 'He's a
kind old fellow!'

Everyone cycled home, eager to tell their
mothers about the morning's meeting. Peter and
Janet went to find the mattress in the loft. Yes,
there it was, rolled up in thick brown paper, and
tied with string. They dragged it to the trap-
door of the loft, and let it slide down the ladder
– BUMP! It landed at the bottom very suddenly
and Scamper tore down the stairs in a great
fright.

Mother went to her linen cupboard, and her
blanket store, and found two old sheets and a
blanket, warm and cosy. She chose a saucepan
from the kitchen, and a teapot and jug from the
dresser there. She rummaged out an old oil-

stove too, to air the caravan.

Peter and Janet carried everything to the hall, and stored it there ready for when the farm-van called that afternoon, as Mother had arranged.

Just before half-past two the other Secret Seven members arrived, each with a list or some notes scribbled in a notebook.

Nobody forgot the password this time, and Scamper was really very funny when they all arrived at the shed. He said 'Wuff' before they did!

Peter collected the lists, and read them over. 'Gosh – your mothers have been really generous!' he said, pleased. 'Everyone's offered a blanket – and our mother did too. Let's take the lists to her, and let her decide which things will be best for the caravan. At this rate we'd have enough to furnish a dozen caravans!'

They took the lists to Peter's mother, and she

checked them quickly with a pencil, crossing off duplicated articles.

'This is fine!' she said. 'Did you arrange to have the things ready, all of you?'

'Oh yes,' said everyone.

'Very well – I think I can hear the farm-van outside now,' said Peter's mother. 'We'll pack our own things into it – and then collect what we want from the other houses. Come along!'

It was fun going round in the van and collecting so many things. Everyone's mother was very kind, and said that they were pleased to think that the Secret Seven was doing such a fine job.

'And now we'll drive up to the old caravan,' said Peter's mother. 'And really set to work! We're going to have some fun!'

CHAPTER SIX

An afternoon of hard work!

'DID SUSIE and Binkie try to interfere, Jack, when you asked your mother for a list of things she could spare?' said Janet.

'Oh yes – and they were very cross when I said it was Secret Seven business,' said Jack. 'I told Susie there was nothing to stop her saving up a bit of money and buying something on her own. But she always wants to butt in on the Secret Seven!'

'I think perhaps you might have let them, just for once,' said Peter's mother.

'But, Mother – you don't understand,' said Peter at once. 'If we let Susie in just ONCE we'd never get rid of her. And, anyhow, we don't want eight people. We're the Secret *Seven*.'

The farm-van stopped at a field-gate, and

Peter jumped down to open it. A grassy road led round the hill to where old Matt the shepherd had his hut and kept his sheep.

The van jolted slowly over the rough road, and the kettle and saucepans rattled and clanked inside. Everyone was sitting on the two old mattresses and blankets – it was quite comfortable! At last the van jolted to a stop, and the driver called out, 'We're as near the caravan as I can get. And here comes old Matt.'

The shepherd opened the door of the van and smiled all over his face as he looked inside and saw so many people.

'Why, you've all come,' he said. 'That's very kind of you! And what a lot of goods! That old caravan won't know itself. I've been cleaning it up a bit, but it's still pretty dirty.'

'We'll soon make it nice and clean!' said Janet, jumping out. 'Come on, Mother!'

How hard they all worked that afternoon! They washed and scrubbed and swept. Peter mended two shelves to hold pots and pans. George stacked the mattresses neatly rolled up, inside the caravan. 'It will be quite easy for Mrs Bolan to untie them tonight!' he said.

Matt came back again about two hours after. He had been rounding up some of the sheep, and his old dog was with him. Scamper ran to him to play, but the sheepdog lay down, put his nose down between his paws, and shut his eyes.

'He can't be bothered with you, Scamper!' said Peter, grinning at the surprised spaniel. 'No – leave him alone. He's run for miles, getting the sheep in, and he's tired. Matt – have you been able to tell the Bolans about this caravan yet?'

'Yes, I have,' said Matt. 'They were that pleased. Mrs Bolan wouldn't believe it at first. I didn't tell her you were going to furnish it, though. I thought that would be a nice surprise. She'll be along any time now.'

'Well – we've just about finished,' said Peter. 'Come and look, Matt.'

Matt could hardly believe his eyes when he saw the spick-and-span caravan, looking so cosy inside. He stared in wonder.

'There now – who'd have thought it?' he said. 'And your father talked of chopping it up for firewood next winter!'

'There's Mrs Bolan, look – with the old

pram!' said Janet. 'And the little boy. She's got something piled on the pram – two loaves of bread and a few parcels. Oh, poor things, of course, all their food was burnt too! We never thought of bringing any for them!'

'Yes, we did,' said George. 'My mother sent a few tins. I've put them on the shelves that Peter mended. I expect Mrs Bolan will be sure to have brought milk for the baby.'

'We could get the shepherd to bring up milk each morning,' said Peter. 'Couldn't we, Mother?'

Mrs Bolan wheeled the pram towards them,

looking surprised and a little scared to see so many people outside the old caravan. She smiled nervously. Matt went up to her in his slow, kindly way, speaking to her as if she were one of his nice old sheep.

'Come along now, Mrs Bolan, don't you be afraid, we're all friends here. This is the caravan you can have, and they've worked hard to make it really cosy. Take a look inside.'

Peter's mother came forward. 'We were so sorry to hear of the fire last night,' she said. 'Oh, what a dear little baby! And what's the little boy's name?'

But as soon as Benny felt her hand on his head he turned and fled away, hands outstretched in front of him, stumbling as he went. Janet started after him.

'Leave him be,' called Mrs Bolan. 'He's so scared now, poor lamb, what with the fire and all!'

Janet stopped. The boy, about eight years old, was small for his age, and looked a little strange. He had enormous dark eyes that stared rather blankly at them, and a shock of very black, curly hair round his small brown face. He made his way into a bush and crouched there, peering out like a small animal, listening to everything that was said.

Mrs Bolan was now admiring the caravan. 'Why, there's everything we want!' she said, looking round in pleasure. 'Even tins on the shelf! And clean as a new pin too! It's really kind of you to do all this for me. I cried my eyes out last night when that old shack of ours went up – a nasty place it was, cold and draughty, but it was our home.'

'When's your husband coming?' asked Peter, hoping to see Luke's pleasure too.

'Oh Luke – Luke's real upset,' said Mrs Bolan, looking worried. 'We lost a few precious things in that fire, you see. I lost my sewing-machine, and Luke lost his banjo and . . .'

'Oh – does he play the banjo?' said Colin. 'So does my uncle. What a pity it was burnt.'

The baby began to cry, and Mrs Bolan bent over her. 'I must give her some milk,' she said, 'and then I'll settle into the van. My, we're lucky. I'll send Luke down to thank you properly as soon as I can.'

'Shall we go now?' said Peter, and his mother nodded. She turned to Matt.

'You can bring up some milk for the baby

each day, can't you, Matt?' she said to the kindly old shepherd, and he nodded.

'Well, good-bye then, Mrs Bolan,' said Peter, and everyone called out some little message too. 'Good luck! We hope the caravan will be comfortable! Tell us if there's anything else we can do!'

Peter went over to where Benny was hiding. 'Good-bye, Benny,' he said, but the strange little boy didn't answer. His great dark eyes wandered up to Peter's face, and yet Peter felt as if he was not really looking at him. What a curious child!

CHAPTER SEVEN

Susie and Binkie are a nuisance

As THE Secret Seven went down the hill in the farm-van, glad to have done a really good job, they saw a man in the distance, walking slowly up. 'I bet that's Luke Bolan,' said Janet. 'I hope he'll be pleased when he sees what we've done for him.'

'I expect he will,' said her mother. 'But you must remember that even though he has a roof over his head now, he and Mrs Bolan have lost every one of their possessions – except that old pram! And it's a terrible thing to lose things you have had for years and years – like Luke's banjo.'

'Are they expensive?' asked Jack.

'Good gracious yes!' said Colin. 'My uncle paid a mint of money for his!' And he began to pretend that he was playing a banjo, strumming with his fingers and making a banjo-like noise that made everyone laugh.

'Do we have another meeting soon?' asked Barbara. 'I wish we could. It was nice to have the two we've just had.'

'Well, let's,' said Peter. 'Even though there isn't anything to have a meeting about, we could talk and have a bit of fun. Mother, can we get out of the van now and walk over the fields? It's such a nice afternoon.'

'Yes – and if you'd all like to come back afterwards to a late tea, I'll have it ready for you,' said his mother. 'You really have worked very hard, and you must be getting hungry already! I'll telephone to tell the other mothers.'

'Oh, Mother! You really are a pet!' said Janet, and everyone agreed. 'Of course we'd like tea – what shall we have? Eggs? Ham?'

'Wait and see,' said her mother, laughing. 'Well, out you all get, and I'll drive on alone. Good-bye for an hour or two!'

The Seven leapt out of the van, Scamper too, and set off across the fields. It was a wonderful spring day, with the birds singing madly and primroses everywhere. Cowslips nodded on the hillsides too, and celandines shone out from the ditches.

'They're so shining-bright that they look as if they've been polished,' said Barbara.

A voice suddenly hailed them, and the Seven stopped. 'Ahoy there! Wait for us!'

'Bother! It's Susie and Binkie,' said Jack in disgust. Sure enough it was – and they came leaping down the hill at top speed.

'Hallo! What happened about the caravan?' yelled Susie.

They told her, and she and Binkie listened with interest. 'You might have let us help!' said Susie reproachfully. 'Even though we don't belong to the Secret Seven.'

'Well, we said you could buy the Bolans anything you wanted to,' said Janet. 'Why don't you? You could take it up to the caravan yourselves.'

45

'Well, we jolly well will,' said Susie. 'Can we come with you now, or are you the high-and-mighty Secret Seven again, all on your own?'

'Don't be an idiot,' said Peter. 'You can see we're not holding a meeting just at this moment, so of course you can come with us.'

'Binkie's made up a poem,' said Susie, with a sudden little giggle. 'All about the Secret Seven.'

'Well, we don't want to hear it,' said George, feeling quite certain that it wouldn't be a very polite one.

'It's got a chorus,' said Susie. 'Hasn't it, Binkie? Let Binkie say the poem, Peter, and we can all join in the chorus.'

'Don't you let her, Peter,' said Jack, at once. 'You've no idea how rude Susie and Binkie can get when they put their heads together.'

But Susie was not going to be stopped, nor Binkie either. Binkie began to chant lines in a loud, sing-song manner, dancing about in front of them.

'Oh see the Secret Seven
So very smug and pi,
Eyes turned up to Heaven,

46

When they come walking by!
They think they're very clever,
Alas, we don't agree,
We think the Secret Seven
Are silly as can be!

'*Chorus, please* . . .' And here Susie joined in
at the top of her voice –

'Silly as can be, Silly as—'

But that was too much for the Secret
Seven. With one accord they ran at the irritating
Binkie and the aggravating Susie, yelling
loudly.

'How dare you make up that song! Shut up!
You horrible girl! Be quiet! We'll . . .'

But Susie and Binkie were racing away at top
speed, laughing at the anger of the Secret Seven.
'Serves you right for not letting us help this
afternoon!' yelled Susie, stopping for a moment.
'You just look out for us! We'll pay you back
for that!'

Then off they raced again. 'I thought this
would happen,' said Jack gloomily. 'I'm very
sorry about it – but I can't help having Susie

for my sister. As for Binkie – think what you'd all feel like if you had to have a girl like her staying a whole week with you!'

'It's a very rude and untruthful song,' said Barbara, who always hated being made fun of.

'It's just a *little* bit funny too,' said George, but nobody would agree with him. They were now walking beside a field where a scarecrow stood, and stopped to have a look at him. A rook stood on his old black hat, and he looked very comical.

The wind waved his torn old tweed coat about and made him seem alive. 'He's got Daddy's old trousers on,' said Janet, with a laugh. 'The ones Mummy didn't like because they were too light and showed the dirt so much. And someone's tied a dirty scarf round his neck. It looks like the onc our cowman used to wear – red with white spots!'

The rook bent over the scarecrow's face and pecked it. 'Shoo!' shouted Peter indignantly. 'You're supposed to be scared of him. Shoo, rook, shoo!'

The rook gave two loud caws that sounded exactly as if it was laughing, spread its big black wings and flew off slowly, cawing as it went.

'I bet it's saying something rude – like Binkie,' said George. 'I say, I'm awfully hungry now. What about that tea your mother promised us, Peter?'

That made them all hurry off at once. Eggs, ham, cold sausages, cheese, a fruit cake – they could eat the whole lot. So could Scamper. WUFF-WUFF!

CHAPTER EIGHT

Matt has surprising news

THE TEA was ready by the time the Seven poured into the farm-house. They washed and made themselves tidy and then settled down happily at the table. What a spread!

'Cream cheese!' said Jack, in delight.

'Ham and eggs!' said Pam hungrily. 'My favourite!'

'Now just help yourselves,' said Peter's mother, smiling round. 'You deserve a treat after all your good work this afternoon. I saw your sister Susie and that friend of hers as I came home, Jack, and nearly asked them in too.'

'Mother! What an *awful* idea!' said Peter, helping himself to two cold sausages, a hard-boiled egg and a slice of ham. 'That girl Binkie made up a very rude song about us. If you'd

asked her in she might quite well have had the
nerve to sing it at the tea-table.'

'I'd throw the cream cheese at her if she did,'
said Jack, quite fiercely.

'Oh no you wouldn't,' said Peter's mother at
once. 'I don't make cream cheese for that kind
of thing. Colin, you haven't taken nearly enough
ham.'

'He's dreaming!' said Pam, giving him a
nudge. 'Wake up, Colin – whatever are you
thinking of?'

'Well, actually, I suddenly thought of a sort
of poem about Binkie,' said Colin, blinking his
eyes suddenly, as if he were coming out of a
dream.

'A poem! Surely *you* don't write poems,
Colin!' said Janet, amazed. 'How does it
begin?'

'Well, it begins like this,' said Colin, and then changed his mind. 'No, I'd better not tell you.'

That made everyone press him all the more, of course, and at last he grinned and recited a few lines, a little afraid that Peter's mother, who was listening, might not approve.

'Oh Binkie has the habit.
Of a funny little rabbit,
Twitching up and down her little nose . . .'

The next line was lost in gales of laughter. 'Oh Colin – that's *exactly* Binkie!' cried Jack in delight. 'I shall recite it to her whenever she and Susie start that awful Secret Seven song.'

'How does it go on, Colin?' asked Janet, looking at him in admiration.

'Well, I've only got as far as two more lines,' said Colin.

'And in her mouth beneath
Are little rabbit teeth . . .

I can't think of the last line yet!'

'It doesn't sound awfully kind,' said Peter's

mother, and that made Colin go red and say no more.

'Well, but Susie and Binkie aren't kind either,' argued Janet. 'Let's think of a last line:

> 'And in her mouth beneath,
> Are little rabbit teeth . . .'

'No, don't,' said Colin, anxious not to displease Janet's mother. He frowned hard at Janet, and tried to kick her under the table, but only succeeded in kicking poor Scamper, who gave a loud and indignant yelp.

'Oh sorry, Scamper, sorry!' said Colin, and slid under the table to comfort Scamper – and to change the subject too!

'Well, that was a simply delicious tea, Mother,' said Peter when the meal at last came to an end. 'I wish I could begin all over again, but I can't.'

'It's funny – but when I tasted that cream cheese at the beginning of the meal I thought it was just about the nicest thing in the world,' said Pam. 'But now I can't even bear to look at it!'

'We'll help wash up,' said Barbara.

'Oh thanks,' said Janet. 'Shall we *all* wash

up, Mother? We'll be very, very careful.'

'Yes. That would be nice of you,' said her mother, and took up her mending while the Seven went in and out, taking the dirty dishes to the kitchen.

'We'll have a meeting tomorrow, if everyone approves,' said Peter, wiping the dishes carefully. 'Can you all come at ten?'

'No. I've got to go on errands,' said Pam. 'I could come at eleven though.'

It turned out that eleven o'clock was all right for everyone, so it was duly arranged. 'We'll have to have a different password,' said Peter, 'because Susie and Binkie know the last one.'

'Wuff,' said Scamper, looking up.

'Yes, that's right. You really are too clever for words, Scamper!' said Peter, grinning. 'Well – you can choose the next one. Go on – tell us what you'd like.'

'Thump, thump, thump,' went Scamper's tail

on the floor, as he looked up happily at Peter. He did so love being talked to.

'Thank you, Scamper. "Thump" is our next password,' said Peter gravely, and everyone laughed. 'I don't somehow think anyone will forget that!'

Nobody did, of course, and next morning when the knocks came on the closed shed door, where Peter and Janet awaited the others, the password was said at once. 'Thump!'

And each time it was said Scamper thumped his tail joyfully on the floor of the shed. He had never chosen the password himself before, and he felt very, very proud!

Soon all the Seven were sitting down in the shed, talking. They wondered how the Bolans were getting on in their caravan. They wondered if Matt had remembered to take up a bottle of milk when he called for his own that morning. Then George asked Jack if Susie and Binkie knew he had come to the meeting.

'No. I slipped off when they were climbing trees in the garden,' said Jack. 'They keep *on* singing that silly song about us. I tried to remember the one that Colin made up about Binkie, but I couldn't. How does it go, Colin?'

But before Colin could tell him, someone came up to their door and rapped on it.

'Who's there?' called Peter. 'You can't come in unless you know the password. We're holding a meeting.'

'It's me, Matt the shepherd,' said a voice, and Peter opened the door at once. Matt stood there, looking rather cross.

'Have any of you been taking the clothes off that old scarecrow I dressed out in the field for your father?' he said. 'The crows are down there in their hundreds! They don't take fright at a turnip head and sticks – it's only when a scarecrow's dressed and looks like a man that they keep away.'

'No. No, of course we haven't taken the clothes!' said Peter, astonished. 'We wouldn't dream of it!'

'Well – you see if you can find out who did it!' said Matt. 'I'll have to tell your father about it this evening. You just find out for me, will you?' And away he tramped, leaving the Seven too astonished for words. Now, WHO would do a silly thing like that?

CHAPTER NINE

Crash!

THE SECRET Seven looked at each other in astonishment. 'Why, we saw the old scarecrow yesterday,' said Peter. 'There was a rook on his head – so the birds can't be as scared of him as old Matt said!'

'But who could have taken the clothes?' said Jack. 'I mean – they were pretty old and torn, weren't they?'

'Well, the scarecrow has worn them for a long time,' said Janet. 'I wouldn't have thought they were much good for *any*one!'

'They wouldn't be worth a single penny,' said Peter. 'I must say I'm surprised at Matt thinking *we*'d had anything to do with it!'

'Well, we did once do something silly with a scarecrow,' said Janet. 'Don't you remember?

57

We planted some seeds in our own little gardens, and when the birds came and pecked them up we fetched an old scarecrow out of the wheat-field and stood him in the middle of our own seeds! Daddy was very cross – but Mother said we hadn't meant any harm, we were too little then to understand.'

The others laughed at the picture of Janet and Peter dragging a scarecrow all the way to their own small gardens. 'All the same – I expect that's why Matt thought it was you,' said Colin.

'I suppose – I suppose it couldn't be Susie and Binkie, could it?' asked George.

Everyone thought it was very likely! 'It's just the silly sort of thing they *would* do,' said Jack. 'They would think it very, very funny – and they'd know we'd be questioned and feel really puzzled.'

'Well – you'd better ask Susie about it,' said Peter to Jack. 'And if she starts giggling and won't say anything, just say you'll report to *us* and we'll take the matter in hand, as we have been asked to find the clothes.'

'Yes. That sounds very official,' said Jack approvingly. 'I must say it would be a good idea if Colin finished his poem about Binkie, and even made one up about Susie. Those two want taking down a peg.'

'Well, to change the subject,' said Peter. 'Does anyone want to go to the cinema tonight? Janet and I are going, and we'd love to have some of the Secret Seven with us.'

'I can't come,' said Jack. 'If I ask about it, Mother will say that Susie and Binkie are to go too. And I'm *not* going to sit beside two giggly girls all evening.'

'And I can't come,' said Pam. 'Barbara and I are going out to tea with a friend.'

'I could come,' said Colin, and George nodded his head too. 'That would be four of us. We'll meet you at the cinema, five minutes before the film starts. What about the scarecrow clothes now? Do we bother to look about for them, or not?'

'Not till Jack has asked Susie and Binkie if they know anything,' said Peter, getting up. 'Well, that's the end of this meeting. I'll let you all know when there's another. I wish something exciting would happen – *not* like that horrid fire, though!'

That evening Janet and Peter met the other

two at the cinema, paid for their tickets, and went in. It was a good film, and they all enjoyed it. They sat it out to the end and then left the cinema. It was a very dark night, with not a star to be seen.

Peter and Janet were on bicycles, but the other two were walking. 'Good-bye!' said the two cyclists and went off in the darkness, their lamps sending a wavering light in front of them.

Colin and George walked off slowly, talking as they went. All the shops were shut, but some were still lighted, so that, although shut, their goods might still be displayed to any passer-by. The boys looked into them as they passed.

The bicycle shop was lighted up, and they stopped to admire the new racing bicycle in the middle of the window. The next lighted shop was an antique shop, which sold all kinds of interesting things – old pictures, ornaments, tea-sets, musical instruments, chairs and other furniture.

The boys stopped to look at a picture of a long-ago battle, and then walked on again. At the corner Colin suddenly exclaimed, in panic, 'Hey – I believe I've lost my watch. Bother! I

shall get into a row. Do you mind if we walk back and look for it, George? I might have dropped it in the cinema, of course.'

The boys turned and went back very slowly, George's torch lighting up the pavement, as they hunted for the watch. And then the torch flickered faintly – and went out, leaving them in black darkness.

'Look at that now – the battery's gone just when we needed the torch!' groaned Colin.

'Why didn't I bring mine as well? We can't look for the watch in this darkness, that's certain.'

Someone passed them, walking softly in the road, not seeing the two boys standing still on the dark pavement, messing about with the useless torch. He passed so silently that the boys jumped.

'He walked as quietly as a policeman!' said George. 'Gosh – what about going after him, and if he *is* a policeman, we'll report the loss of your watch – then if anyone takes it to the police station it will be returned to you at once – before you get into a row about it!'

'Good idea!' said Colin, and they went after the silent passer-by. They could just make him out in the distance as he passed a lighted shop.

They were almost up to him as he came near to the lighted antique shop, and were just about to call out to him, when he stopped and looked all round him in a curiously cautious manner.

'He's not a policeman after all,' said Colin. 'Hey – what's he doing?'

Things then happened very quickly indeed! The man took something from beneath his coat and threw it at the lighted window of the old antique shop!

CRASH!

The glass splintered at once, and fragments flew all about, glittering in the light from the shop window. The horrified boys saw the man snatch at something in the window and then race off with it at top speed.

He passed by them, and Colin put out a foot to stop him. But the man swerved and raced on, passing under a nearby lamp-post, and then disappearing into the night.

'After him!' shouted George, and they tore round the corner where the man had gone. But he was nowhere to be seen in the darkness – and certainly could not be heard for his tread had been absolutely silent.

What excitement there was then! The crash of breaking glass brought people flocking into the street, shouting and calling. A policeman appeared as if by magic – and someone ran out of the antique shop, joining in the clamour. Good gracious! Colin and George had certainly got something to tell the Secret Seven!

CHAPTER TEN

Very surprising

COLIN AND George ran up to the antique shop. The little man who owned it was wringing his hands as he saw his smashed windows, and everything inside covered with broken glass.

'What's all this?' said the big policeman, looming up silently, and taking out a notebook. 'Who did this?'

'A man,' said someone. 'I just caught sight of him across the road. I couldn't tell you what he was like, though. He raced off at once.'

'What's been taken, sir?' said the policeman to the shopkeeper.

'Oh, that I can't say till I've had a good look,' said the man. 'My word – that picture's done for – that battle picture. The flying glass has cut it to bits – and the brick has smashed that lovely old vase. I don't rightly know what was in the window, sir, till I ask my assistant. He did the window for me yesterday, when I was away. Oh my word, what a mess!'

There was quite a crowd now, round the shop, and soon another policeman came. Colin and George wondered if they ought to say that they, too, had seen the man smash the window, and were just screwing up their courage to do so, when one of the policemen saw that there were a few children in the crowd.

'You get off home,' he said sternly. 'Go on now. You can't help us, you only hinder us. Clear off!'

Colin and George slipped away at once. They had seen all they wanted to, and they were pretty sure that they couldn't give much help. Also, they didn't much like the thought of being stared at by so many people if they went up to the policemen and spoke to them. Why, some of them might think that they had smashed the window, and were owning up!

'We MUST get Peter to call a meeting tomorrow and tell the Secret Seven about this,' panted George as they ran home. 'I don't expect we can *do* anything. But I think we *ought* to tell the others.'

Colin agreed. Anyway, it would be most exciting to relate the story to them! How he wished he and George had managed to trip the man up, and perhaps catch him. What a thrill *that* would have been!

Colin telephoned to Peter the next morning. 'Peter – is that you? Listen, George and I saw a thief smash a window coming home from the cinema last night and steal something out of the antique shop. We actually *saw* the man. Do you think we could have a meeting about it? It's really very exciting.'

'Gosh – did you actually *see* him?' said Peter. 'Dad heard about it from his cowman, and told us at breakfast – and Janet and I groaned because we thought we'd been just too early to see it happen.'

'Well, we had to go back to see if we could find my watch,' said Colin. 'If we hadn't done that we'd have missed all the excitement. What time shall we come to the meeting, Peter? George and I can go round and tell the others now, if you like.'

'Right. Well, bring them along as soon as possible,' said Peter. 'Janet and I will be waiting down in the shed.'

It was quite an excited group of children who met in the shed some time later. All of them had heard of the smashing of the window, but nobody except Pam knew what had been stolen.

She listened quietly to the story told by Colin and George, as did the others. Peter and Janet wished that Colin had discovered that his watch was missing before he had said goodbye to them – then they, too, would have seen the excitement.

'Actually,' said Colin, 'I *hadn't* lost my watch, after all! I found it on my dressing-table when I got home!'

'*Did* you?' said George. 'Gosh – and to think

how we searched every inch of the pavement! By the way, does anyone know if the man has been caught yet?'

'Not so far,' said Peter. 'My father had to see the police this morning about a dog that's worrying our sheep – and the policeman told him they hadn't the foggiest idea who the thief was – or why the man wanted to steal anything from the antique shop. Dad didn't hear what was stolen, however. Does anyone know?'

'Yes, *I* know,' said Pam at once. 'It was a very, very old violin, worth thousands of pounds! It was in the very front of the window, with a card telling its history. The man took that, and the bow too!'

'Ah – he must be a violinist, then,' said Peter, saying what everyone was thinking. 'They'll be checking on all the local violinists, I expect.'

'I hope they won't question Miss Hilbrun, the violin teacher at our school!' said Pam. 'She's a wonderful player – but I'm sure she would go into a dead faint if a policeman wanted to ask her questions. She even had to go and sit down for half an hour once, in the middle of teaching, because someone let the piano-lid drop with a bang!'

'I bet you were the one that did that,' said Jack.

'I was not. It was your sister Susie,' said Pam. 'You might have guessed that! Oh dear – it really makes me smile to think of our mouse-like Miss Hilbrun throwing a brick into a window to steal a violin!'

'Listen, George and Colin,' said Peter. 'According to the policeman Dad spoke to this morning when he was reporting that dog, nobody seemed to know exactly how the man was dressed or what he looked like. Did *you* happen to notice? You ought to have done, because that's one of the rules of the Secret Seven – always to be observant, and keep our eyes open.'

'Well – yes – I think I can tell you more or

less what he looked like,' said George, though Colin looked rather blank. 'I can't say that I actually noted it all – but I did get a very good view of him in the bright light from the window, just as he smashed it – a sort of quick photograph of him in my mind, if you know what I mean.'

'Tell us, then,' said Peter, taking out his notebook. 'It might be really useful. We could look out for him if we know, for instance, what he's wearing.'

'Well – he was medium size,' said George, half-shutting his eyes to picture the man in his mind. 'And he had a very torn old coat of brown tweed – *very* torn. And trousers that were a kind of light grey and very dirty. And a black hat with a hole in it. And, oh yes – a scarf round his neck with red-and-white spots.'

Peter gave a loud exclamation. 'George! Do you know what you've just described EXACTLY? The clothes that were stolen from the *scarecrow*!'

CHAPTER ELEVEN

A very interesting meeting

THE SECRET Seven stared at Peter in the utmost amazement. What! The violin thief had been dressed in the clothes stolen from the scarecrow? But WHY?

'You don't suppose it was the *scarecrow* who stole out in the night and took the violin, do you?' said Pam, with one of her sudden giggles.

'Don't be silly. You know the scarecrow hasn't any clothes now – unless Matt has found some more for him,' said Janet.

'This is very, very interesting,' said Peter slowly. 'It certainly rules out jokers like Susie or Binkie.'

'Well, I *did* ask them,' said Jack, 'and honestly I couldn't make out whether they knew anything about the scarecrow's clothes or not, they giggled so. I half thought they *did*, as a matter of fact.'

'Well, they couldn't have. They were just pulling your leg,' said Peter. 'Now let's think carefully about this, and if anyone has a sensible remark, please make it. We know two things – one, that a man stole a very valuable old violin last night – and two, that for some reason he wore old clothes belonging to a scarecrow. Now what do we make of that?'

'Well, if the violin was old and valuable, and was obviously the one thing he had made up his mind to steal, it's clear that he must have been a violinist himself, or know about the value of old ones,' said Colin at once. 'The odds are that he is a musician, if not a violinist.'

'And he wore those awful old clothes as a disguise so that if he were seen he couldn't possibly be recognised,' said Barbara.

'And he didn't want to buy them at an old clothes shop or borrow them from any tramp, in case of questions being asked,' said Jack.

'So he spotted our scarecrow and took the clothes from *him*!' said Peter. 'And presumably he will throw them away now or hide them somewhere.'

'He might put them on the scarecrow again,' suggested George.

'No. He'd be afraid that it might be watched,' said Peter. 'Anyway, it's sure to be dressed up again now. No – he'll either burn or bury those clothes.'

'We could look for them – only we'd probably never find them!' said Janet. 'I mean – there's the whole countryside to hide them in!'

'Yes, that's true,' said Peter. 'Well – has anyone any other suggestion?'

Nobody had. It seemed impossible to hunt for a violinist they didn't know who had been dressed in clothes he had probably already hidden away!

'Do we know any first-class violinists who would love a valuable old violin?' asked Pam hopefully.

'Well, yes we do,' said Peter, 'but none of them would dress up in scarecrow clothes and smash a shop-window. I mean, there's old Mr Scraper at school, who teaches the violin – but I can't possibly imagine him doing things like that. Or Mr Luton, our churchwarden – he plays the violin too, so does his wife. But they wouldn't go about smashing windows. No – it must be someone a bit mad, I think, who has an urge to steal and use a really precious old violin.'

'But yet sensible enough to use the scarecrow's clothes as a disguise!' said Jack.

'Yes. Well, it's a puzzle. I don't really see that there's anything we can do to solve it at the moment,' said Peter. 'Except look out for old clothes stuffed in a ditch or a bush, or buried somewhere.'

Scamper suddenly began to bark loudly, and everyone looked up. 'I bet that's Susie,' said Jack, in disgust. 'We've got to go and see my granny this morning, and Susie said she'd call for me here. I *told* her not to! Interrupting our meeting!'

The rude Secret Seven song came on the air at that moment, sung lustily by two voices – Susie's and Binkie's.

'Oh see the Secret Seven,
So very smug and pi,
Eyes turned up to Heaven,
When they come walking by!
They think . . .'

Colin flew to the door and opened it. He sang at the top of *his* voice – and he had a really loud one –

'Oh Binkie has the habit
Of a silly little rabbit,
Twitching up and down her little nose!
And in her mouth beneath
Are lots of rabbit teeth
And that's the way a little Binkie grows!'

The Secret Seven listened in delight. That would serve Binkie right for making up such a horrid poem about *them*! They hadn't heard the end of the poem before, because Colin had only thought of it that very minute!

Susie marched right up to Colin, red in the face with anger.

'You've made Binkie cry with that song!' she said. 'How dare you? I'll pay you back, you Secret Seven, for making up such an unkind song about my best friend.'

'Well, Binkie started it, with her rude Secret Seven song,' said Colin stoutly. But all the same he felt rather ashamed of making Binkie cry. Perhaps it *was* rather an unkind song.

'Jack, you're to come now,' ordered Susie. 'Granny will be waiting for us.'

'All right, all right. Don't order me about,' said Jack. He turned to the others. 'What about this afternoon?' he said. 'Are we going anywhere?'

'We might go up and have a look to see how the gingerbread woman, Mrs Bolan, is getting on in her caravan,' said Peter. 'Mother has given us some baby clothes to take up, and I thought I'd take my old toy bus for Benny.'

'Right. I'll be along about half-past two. Is that all right?' asked Jack.

'Make it three,' said Peter, and the others nodded. 'We'll keep an eye open for scarecrow clothes on the way,' he added, lowering his voice.

'*I* heard you,' said Susie, at once. 'And what's more, I know you and the others think that Binkie and I were the idiots who took the scarecrow clothes, but we didn't. Jack asked us about them. It's just about time you Secret Seven made a mistake about something! You think you're too clever for words. So look out – else you'll be sorry!' And away she went with Binkie.

'Now what exactly does she mean by *that*?' said Peter.

CHAPTER TWELVE

Scamper makes a find

AT ABOUT three o'clock that afternoon the Secret
Seven set off through the fields to go to visit the
Bolans' caravan. Scamper raced along with
them as usual.

'We shall pass the scarecrow on the way,'
said Colin. 'I wonder what he's wearing now?'

He was fully dressed again, in a curious
collection of clothes. He wore a woman's hat
with a feather in – a raincoat full of holes, and
old macintosh trousers, very torn. He stood
there looking rather forlorn and ashamed of
himself.

Janet gave a squeal of laughter when she saw
his hat.

'That's the hat that the cowman's wife used
to wear in church!' she said. 'I've often and

often watched that feather waggling in it when she fell asleep on a hot Sunday!'

'And those trousers belong to the cowman,' said Peter. 'He must have got a new pair. I think the macintosh is the shepherd's. Well – the old scarecrow looks peculiar now, doesn't he? Hi, Scarecrow! Where are your other clothes?'

The scarecrow flapped his sleeves dismally and didn't answer! They left him standing sadly in the field, and went on towards the Bolans' caravan, up by Matt the shepherd's hut.

On the way they had to pass over a small bridge across a gurgling stream. Scamper, hearing the water, ran joyfully ahead. Now he could get a drink!

But he stopped before he came to the little

stream and began to sniff in a ditch in the greatest excitement.

'What's up, Scamper?' called Peter. 'What are you scrabbling at?'

Scamper was certainly excited. He barked, and scraped vigorously with his front paws. The Secret Seven came up to him and looked down in amusement. Then Janet gave a little cry.

'Peter! Look – what's that sticking out of the hole he's made? It looks like a bit of cloth. Oh, PETER! It couldn't be the scarecrow clothes, could it?'

'Well – this does look a bit like old grey flannel – and we know that the scarecrow's trousers *were* flannels!' said Peter, feeling a little surge of excitement welling up inside him. 'Go on, Scamper. Find it, then, find it!'

Scamper scraped at top speed, flinging out earth behind him, and covering the Seven with it. Soon he had got firm hold of whatever was there, and tugged it right out in triumph.

'Wuff!' he said. 'Wuff, wuff, wuff!'

Peter picked up the piece of grey flannel. It didn't look like trousers. It looked more like a torn piece of skirt. He looked down at Scamper, who

was busy burrowing
again in the hole he
had made, giving little
whines of excitement.

'He's got something

else there,' said Jack. 'Maybe the old hat.'

Yes – in half a minute Scamper brought up
an old hat – but what a hat! It was a very old
straw one, with a ribbon round it – a ribbon that
Pam recognised only too well!

'Peter! That's one of our old school hats and
the school ribbon we wear at our school! This
hat has never been on any scarecrow! Whatever
does it all mean?'

'Wuff!' said Scamper again, in delight, and
put his nose right into the hole he had made. He
brought out a large and extremely smelly bone,

which he proudly laid at Peter's feet.

'Good gracious!' said Peter, amazed. 'So that's why you dug down there – you smelt the bone! But why in the world did anyone bury the . . .'

And just then there came the sound of someone exploding into laughter. What an explosion that was! The Seven turned at once – and there were Susie and Binkie, rolling about on a bank of grass, behind which they had been spying on the excited Seven!

'Oh, I'll die of laughing! Oh, I can't bear it! Oh, Scamper, you're a perfect wonder! Oh, I've got such a stitch in my side!'

That was Susie, of course. She went off into a cascade of laughs again, and Binkie joined her, shouting out just like Susie.

'Oh did you see their faces when they found your old school hat, Susie? Oh, I'm dying of laughing! I can't laugh any more, I'm crying with laughter! Oh, that smelly old bone! Good old Scamper!'

Scamper couldn't make out why Susie and Binkie were rolling about and squealing. He thought they must be hurt, and he put his tail down and ran over to them, whining.

'Come back, Scamper,' said Peter, and Scamper ran back, surprised at Peter's stern voice.

'I suppose you think this is funny,' began Peter, calling to the two girls. 'Well . . .'

'Oh yes, we do think it's funny!' laughed Susie, wiping her eyes. 'The funniest thing that ever happened. You were all so solemn!'

'Oh come on – let's leave them to their silly giggling,' said Jack furiously, and the Seven walked with great dignity to the little stream and crossed the bridge. But after a little while Pam gave a sudden giggle. She looked round apologetically.

'Sorry,' she said. 'But honestly it *was* rather funny.' And she gave another little giggle.

Barbara couldn't help joining in. 'We must have looked funny, poring over a bit of Susie's old school skirt and her old school hat,' she said, and began to laugh.

And then, of course, everyone saw the funny side, and they roared with laughter, just as Susie and Binkie had. Oh dear – how easily they had been taken in!

'It was really rather clever of them to think of burying the bone at the *bottom* of the hole, and putting the other things on top,' said Janet. 'I mean – they must have planned it very well, really. They knew we were coming up here . . .'

'And that old Scamper would smell the bone, and scrape a hole,' said Jack. 'And that we'd get all excited to see the piece of cloth there. Oh dear – we were properly taken in. Well, they've paid us back all right.'

'Here we are, almost at the caravan,' said Peter. 'And there's Mrs Bolan, look, doing some washing outside. Hallo, Mrs Bolan!'

CHAPTER THIRTEEN

An odd little boy

MRS BOLAN looked up as the children came towards her.

'Well, it's nice to see you,' she said, smiling her nice smile. 'Oh – what's that you've brought me? What a lovely little coat – and a little dress too. The baby won't know herself!'

'And I brought this for Benny,' said Peter, producing the bus. 'Where is he?'

'Somewhere about,' said his mother, and called: 'Benny! Where are you, love? Benny, there's a present for you.'

But no Benny appeared. 'He's hiding,' said his mother. 'He's scared of visitors.'

'Doesn't he go to school?' asked Pam, looking all round for the little boy. 'Or is he too young?'

'He's eight,' said Mrs Bolan. 'He's never

84

been to school. He wouldn't like it, and it wouldn't be any good. Poor Benny – he hasn't had much luck in his life. Oh land's sake, look at that baby now, hanging half out of her pram! What I'll do with her when she can walk, I *don't* know. But there, maybe Benny will look after her – he loves his little sister.'

The girls wandered off to look inside the caravan. It looked cosy and comfortable, but not very tidy or very clean.

'Did we give you everything you needed?' asked Janet. 'We tried to think of everything.'

'Yes, love – all except needles and cottons!' said Mrs Bolan, laughing. 'You wouldn't believe how much I've wanted those – to run up little curtains for the windows, and to mend my clothes – these I stand in are the only ones I've got – all the others were burnt.'

'Oh – we never even thought of needles and cottons – or scissors either,' said Janet. 'I expect you wanted scissors too, didn't you, Mrs Bolan?'

'Oh yes – but Luke left me his penknife,' said Mrs Bolan, squeezing out her washing. 'And Matt the shepherd is good to me – he brings me other little things, you know.'

'We'll come up again as soon as we can, Mrs Bolan,' promised Janet, 'and bring you a small work-basket. I never use my old one; you can have that. Is there anything else?'

'Well, I suppose you haven't an old bucket to spare, have you?' asked Mrs Bolan. 'You did bring one, but Benny's gone off with it, bless his heart. He plays little tunes on it with a stick – he's clever at that, and it keeps him happy, poor lamb.'

'Yes, we'll bring you a bucket too,' said Peter. 'As soon as we can. Listen – what's that noise?'

'Oh, that's Benny with his bucket!' said Mrs Bolan. 'Sounds quite like music, doesn't it! Dinga-dinga-dong-dong, dinga-dinga-dong, dong! Benny, you bring me my bucket!'

There was silence after that, and Mrs Bolan shook her head. 'No good going after him,' she said. 'He'll hide himself somewhere, and keep as still as a rabbit in its burrow.'

'Is your husband still down at the fair?' asked Peter.

'The fair's moved on,' she answered. 'Didn't you know? Luke's gone with it. It moved off this morning, and Luke won't be back with me for a few days. I shall miss him, up here alone on the hills. But old Matt there, he keeps coming to see if I'm all right!'

Janet thought she was a brave, cheerful and generous little woman. She remembered how she had given them a batch of her hot ginger-bread at the fair, when they had no money to pay for it.

'There's Benny!' said Jack suddenly, and beckoned to the small boy, who took no notice at all. He had appeared beside some gorse bushes, and stood staring across at them, scarcely blinking his great dark eyes.

'There now – you see he's hidden that bucket of mine somewhere, just as I said!' said Mrs Bolan. 'Benny, you come over here. There's a lovely present for you, a beauty. It's a bus! You come and get it.'

Benny stood quite silent, still staring. The children thought him a very odd little boy indeed, but he was a striking and lovely child, and Janet longed to give him a hug. He began to walk over to them, slowly and carefully, as if afraid of falling. He stopped fairly near and stared towards them again.

Peter went over to him with the bus. He held

it out, but the child made no attempt to take it. So Peter put it gently into his hands, and at once the boy clutched it, and ran his fingers all over it in delight.

When he found the little hooter that said 'Toot-toot!' his whole face lit up and he smiled sweetly.

'Toot-toot-toot!' he sang, in a tuneful little voice. 'It's a bus, Mammy, a bus. Is it for me, Mammy?'

'Yes, for you,' said his mother. 'Say thank you nicely to Peter.'

'Thank you,' said Benny, looking at George, instead of at Peter. Janet thought he had the strangest eyes she had ever seen, dark, beautiful and deep, but without any expression at all.

Scamper ran up and pushed his head against Benny's leg. Benny backed away, half scared, and Peter called Scamper to him. Benny went off to the bushes, carrying his precious bus.

'Goo!' said the baby, bouncing up and down in her pram. 'Goo-goo!' She wanted attention too, and Janet went over to her at once. She was as lively as Benny was quiet. She put her fat little hand against Janet's cheek.

'She likes you,' said Mrs Bolan, smiling.

'Now stop bouncing, you little monkey, or you'll have the springs out of that old pram!'

'It's time to go,' said Peter, looking at his watch. 'Mrs Bolan, we'll bring you a bucket, and needles and cotton and any other little thing we can think of as soon as we can! I'm so glad you like the caravan.'

'Oh, it's fine,' said Mrs Bolan cheerfully. She was now pegging up clothes on a line that stretched from one tree to another. 'Thank you for coming.'

The Seven went off together, with Scamper trotting in front, sniffing at everything. When he came to the hole where the bone had been he remembered that he had left his precious, magnificent bone up at the caravan site, and bounded back to fetch it.

'Well, I'm glad we went up there,' said Janet. 'But Benny puzzles me. What a strange little boy – and I really do think he ought to go to school. He's eight! I'll tell Mother about him, and perhaps she can arrange something.'

'Here comes Scamper again,' said Peter. 'Pooh, take that bone away from me, Scamper – it's the smelliest, nastiest one I've ever known!'

CHAPTER FOURTEEN

Something very strange

TWO DAYS went by, and the Seven were very busy with all kinds of things. Peter and Janet lime-washed the henhouses for their father, with Scamper watching in great interest.

'You look a bit peculiar, Scamper – splashed with white from the lime-wash drips,' said Janet. 'Why *must* you sit exactly under where we're working – you get all the splashes!'

George was busy too, with Colin, rigging a fine ship they had made together. Jack was helping at home. The two girls, Pam and Barbara, were earning a little money by weeding onion beds.

'Horrible job!' Pam told Peter, when she saw him. 'The weeds *will* grow all tangled up with the onion stems, and we keep pulling up tiny onions with the weeds, and have to replant them! Still – we earn fifty pence an hour!'

They often spoke about the stolen violin, especially Colin and George, who spent a good deal of time together on the ship. It was they who had seen the window being smashed, of course, and it was interesting to talk about such an exciting happening.

'It rather looks as if this business about the stolen violin is fading out,' Colin said to George. 'My father asked the police if they'd heard anything about it, or had an idea of who the thief was, but they hadn't.'

'Well, they won't now,' said George. 'The man's gone off with it. I expect he's a hundred miles away!'

Peter and Janet finished their job in the henhouses, and decided to take a day off.

'We think we'll go for a walk, Mother,' said Peter. 'May we have sandwiches?'

'Yes, dear. I'll make you some,' said his mother. 'If you're going near old Matt the shepherd, take him this letter, will you? It didn't come till after he'd fetched his milk this morning.'

'Right,' said Peter. 'We'll go to the woods, I think, and see how far the bluebells are up, and have our picnic there – and then we'll go home over the hill where Matt has his sheep.'

'And we'll look in on the Bolans,' said Janet. 'I love that little baby. Oh, Mother, can you give me an old pair of scissors, please? I promiscd Mrs Bolan I'd take her a pair, and some needles too. You did send a bucket up by Matt, didn't you?'

'No. Matt said she could borrow his,' said Mother. 'Anyhow till that monkey of a boy brings back the bucket we sent before.'

'He's not a monkey at all,' said Janet, remembering the big-eyed, solemn little boy.

'He's a strange little fellow. He only took the bucket to play tunes on!'

The children set off with their sandwiches, Scamper running joyfully ahead. It was a wonderful day again, and the sun was as hot as June. Primroses nestled everywhere, and little wild anemones danced gaily in shady corners. Janet skipped along happily.

'It's lovely to have a day all to ourselves after sticking to that lime-washing job for hour after hour,' she said. 'I wonder if any bluebells will be out. It's terribly early, but you never know.'

The woods were full of springing bluebell leaves, their long green spikes standing guard over the flowers pushing up between them. Janet found one flower right out, its bells a lovely blue.

'Here's one! And another! Oh, I wish we could find a white one. That's so very, very lucky!'

'Better not pick any,' said Peter. 'They would only be dead by the time we get home!'

They had their lunch in the bluebell wood, with the blackbirds and thrushes singing loudly overhead, and a little robin hopping round their feet, waiting for a crumb. Then they went on again, climbing the hills to where Matt the shepherd kept his sheep.

He wasn't in his hut, so they left his letter there, and then went across to where the Bolans had their caravan, a little way off. But that was shut too, and no one was about, not even Benny.

'The sheep are on the opposite hill today,' said Peter, sitting down on the grass. 'What a lot Dad's got now, hasn't he? And how the lambs have grown!'

'It must be rather nice to be a shepherd up on the hills, living by himself with the sheep and the lambs he loves,' said Janet, sitting down beside him. 'Oh look – isn't that old Matt coming up the path over there? And his dog too!'

It was. He smiled when he saw them, and his eyes shone as blue as the sky. Janet wondered why so many people who lived in the open air had such very blue eyes. She ran to meet the old shepherd.

'Well, Janet, it's nice to see you and your dog,' said Matt, leaning on his big crook. 'It isn't often old Matt has visitors. Me and my dog here, we don't see much company.'

'What about the Bolans? You see them, don't you?' asked Peter.

'Oh yes – and Mrs Bolan is a right kind woman,' said Matt. 'I haven't seen her husband. He comes home at odd times, mostly late at night. He works in the fairs, you know. But that boy Benny – he's a strange little fellow, now. Sits and stares at nothing for hours! It's my belief he's not right in the head.'

'Oh dear!' said Janet. 'Perhaps that's why he doesn't go to school, then. Poor little boy.'

'I'd like to set him on my knee and tell him a tale,' said Matt. 'But as soon as he hears anyone coming he's off like a frightened rabbit. I'm wondering if he was scared last night, if he heard what I heard.'

'Why? What did you hear?' asked Peter, in surprise.

'I don't rightly know, Peter,' said Matt, screwing up his wrinkled forehead. 'I was in my hut, half asleep, when I heard it. It was about half-past nine, and a dark night too! What a wailing it was! What a sad, sad noise! It rose up and down, up and down, till I couldn't bear it and went out on the hillside to see if some animal was in pain – and yet it sounded like no living thing. But there was nothing there. As soon as I called out, the wailing stopped.'

Peter and Janet listened in astonishment. What a weird tale! Wailing? Who would be wailing? And why?

'The noise went high and it went low,' said Matt. 'I never did hear such wailing before. It fair went through me, and gripped my heart. I was really glad when it stopped!'

'Do you think it will come tonight?' asked Peter. Matt shook his head.

'How do I know? Maybe – and maybe not. I asked Mrs Bolan about it this morning, and she said she hadn't heard anything. But it was wailing all right!'

'Janet, I'm going to get Jack to come up here and listen with me tonight!' said Peter, as Matt got up to fetch his pipe. 'Wailing! That's something very odd. We'll find out what it is!'

CHAPTER FIFTEEN

Up on the hills at night

PETER AND Janet longed to tell the others this new, strange piece of news. They raced down the hill, with Scamper at their heels.

They passed Jack's house on the way and called in to see him. He was having a jigsaw competition with Susie and Binkie, who at once began to chant the Secret Seven song under their breath. Most annoying!

'Jack, can you spare a moment?' asked Peter. 'We've some rather strange news.'

'What is it?' asked Susie at once, her quick, bird-like eyes staring brightly at Peter.

'I'm afraid it's Secret Seven news,' said Peter coldly. 'Can you come, Jack? You can finish your jigsaw afterwards.'

'Yes, of course,' said Jack, and got up. 'Back

in a few minutes,' he said to Susie and Binkie and marched out with Peter and Janet.

'I'm glad you came,' he said, taking them into another room. 'Mother has made me play with those two girls all day. Oooh – girls! What a bore they are.'

'Thank you very much, Jack,' said Janet indignantly. 'Perhaps I'd better go, and leave you with Peter.'

'No. No, of course not!' said Jack, in alarm. 'I didn't mean *you*. You're fine. It's just those two that get on my nerves.'

Peter snorted. 'Idiots,' he said. 'They must lead you an awful life, Jack. But listen, I want you to do something with me tonight. It's not exactly to do with anything the Secret Seven have been working on, but it's rather strange.'

He told Jack what Matt had said. Jack was amazed. 'He must have been dreaming, don't you think?' he said. 'I mean – what would go wailing out on those hills? If it was an animal, caught in a trap or something, poor thing, old Matt would recognise its wail or howl. If it's something he couldn't place he *must* have been dreaming!'

'I didn't think of that,' said Peter. 'Of course, it might have been a dream – but he said he got up and went out of his hut and still heard it. It stopped when he called out, though.'

'When he woke up, I expect!' said Jack, with a grin.

'Well – perhaps it's not worth bothering about,' said Peter, rather downcast.

'I think it is – and if you don't go, I shall get Pam and Barbara, and we'll go,' said Janet unexpectedly.

The two boys looked at her in surprise.

'No,' said Jack at once. 'It's not right for girls to go by themselves up on the hills at night. I'll go with Peter, of course I will. Shall we ask Colin and George, Peter?'

'Yes. We'll make a sort of adventure of it,' said Peter, pleased. Then, as Janet opened her mouth to argue, he frowned. 'And don't you start asking if you and the other two girls can come, Janet, because you CAN'T!'

'All right, all right,' said Janet, looking rather sulky. How very annoying to be kept out of so many exciting things!

The boys quickly arranged everything. Jack said he would go round and tell Colin and

George, and they would all be outside Peter's front gate as soon as it was dark.

'Bring torches, for goodness' sake,' said Peter. 'There's no moon, and if it's a cloudy night it will be as dark as pitch.'

'Come on – we'd better get back home,' said Janet, looking at her watch. 'We're late for tea already.'

They went quickly out of the room – and heard a stifled giggle. They stopped indignantly.

'Have those two girls been listening?' demanded Peter. 'We shut the door. Surely they aren't mean enough to listen through the keyhole?'

'Susie and Binkie would do *any*thing,' said Jack desperately, and raced after the giggles that could still be heard in the distance.

Peter was very cross, and so was Janet. Why ever hadn't they gone into a corner of the garden, where nobody could possibly hear a word? Well, the only blessing was that they had spoken in fairly low voices, so perhaps Susie and Binkie hadn't heard anything much.

Jack went round to tell Colin and George, and to see if they would like to join in the little adventure. They both laughed at the 'wailing' old Matt had heard, but said they would certainly come.

'We *were* going to the cinema tonight, but we'll come with you and Peter instead,' said Colin.

'Half-past seven outside Peter's front gate,' said Jack. 'No bikes. We'll have to walk up those hills – and let's hope the scarecrow doesn't chase us when we pass his field!'

'It was a funny business about his clothes, wasn't it?' said Colin. 'We never found out anything about those – they just vanished. Right, Jack – you can count on us.'

So, when it was nice and dark, the four boys met outside Peter's gate. Janet was there too, to see them off. 'I *wish* I could come,' she said, still hopeful that she might. But it was no good! The boys said good-bye and strode off up the dark lane, leaving poor Scamper behind too.

It took them some time to get to where old Matt had his hut.

'We won't let him know we're here, in case he's cross about it,' said Peter, in a low voice. 'I vote we sit down behind this bush. I wonder if Matt is in his hut.'

'Yes. I can see a crack of light,' said George. 'He's there all right. Now, we'd better sit absolutely still and quiet, so that the wailer won't guess we're listening or watching.'

So the four boys sat there in utter silence, jumping once when an owl gave a sudden hoot, and straining their ears when some small creature ran over the grass.

And then suddenly the wailing began! Good gracious! What a horrible noise! Woooooo-ooh! Waaaaa-ah! Eeeeeeeeeee! The boys clutched one another, their hearts thumping violently.

'It sounds right behind our bush!' whispered Peter. 'Let's creep round and shine our torches!'

'Woooooo-oooh! Waaaaa-ah! Eeeeeeeee!'

'Now – quick!' said Peter, and round the bush they went.

CHAPTER SIXTEEN

The strange wailing

THE FOUR boys switched on their torches as they stumbled round the great gorse bush – and almost before they got there, they heard another noise – *not* a wail – which filled them with surprise and anger.

They shone their torches on two figures crouching there, both holding their sides with laughter.

'Susie! Binkie! You beasts!' cried Jack, in horror and anger. 'You listened to what Peter said this morning. You've spoilt EVERYTHING!'

'Was our wailing good?' asked Susie, half-choking with laughter. 'Did old Matt hear us too? And the Bolans? We call ourselves the Weird and Wonderful Wailers – did you know?'

A tall figure suddenly looked up in the light of the four torches. It was Matt the shepherd.

'What's this?' he said sternly. 'What are you children doing here at this time of night? What was all that yelling?'

'It wasn't yelling – it was Binkie and me wailing,' said Susie. 'Didn't you hear it last night, Matt?'

'What I heard last night wasn't made by any silly child,' said Matt solemnly. 'You be off before the *real* wailing starts. Yes, all of you. And you, Susie, I'll tell your father of you, so I will. Coming up here in the dark of night!'

'Oh no – please don't tell Dad,' said Susie, really alarmed, and got up in a hurry.

'Come on, Susie,' said Binkie, feeling scared by the stern shepherd. 'Quick!'

And she ran off down the hillside, shining her torch in front of her, Susie following close behind. Jack went after them. 'Wait for me, you idiots. You'll get lost. SUSIE! Wait for me! I'll take you home.'

'You be off too, lads,' said Matt, to the other three. 'If you should hear what *I* heard, you'll be tearing down the hill as if a hundred dogs were after you. Now go. Good night to you.'

And with great dignity the old man walked back to his shack. The boys heard the door shut. They switched off their torches, feeling angry and uncomfortable.

'That Susie!' said George. 'Horrible girl! And Binkie too. Coming up here like that! I must say you were an idiot, Peter, to let Susie overhear what you told Jack.'

'Yes. But honestly you don't expect people to listen at keyholes,' said Peter. 'Though Susie will do anything, of course, to make fun of the Secret Seven. That's all she does it for.'

'Well, shall we push off home too?' asked

Colin. 'I must say this is all very disappointing.'

'We'll wait just a bit – in case the real wailing, that Matt told us about, does happen to come again,' said Peter. 'He said he thought it came about half-past eight – and it's gone that now.'

'Well – five more minutes, then,' said Colin. 'But I'm pretty certain old Matt dreamt it all.'

They sat silently for five minutes, in the pitch-black darkness. Not a star was to be seen in the overclouded sky. An owl hooted again, and the wind made tiny noises in the gorse-bush behind them. Then a bird in a nearby bush unexpectedly gave a little chirrup and was silent again.

'Better go now,' whispered Peter, and rose to his feet. The others stood up too, and Peter took a few steps forward.

Then he stopped very suddenly indeed, and so did the others. Their hearts began to beat fast again, and Colin clutched hold of George.

A strange, sad wailing came on the air – oh how strange and how sad! It rose up through the night, high and full of beauty, and then fell again to a lower note, mournful but still pure and lovely.

Not a sound was to be heard except that strange, unearthly noise. Even the wind seemed to be listening, holding its breath, as were all three boys. They stood transfixed, clutching one another, not making any other movement.

They heard Matt's door open. The old shepherd must have heard the wailing too. It wasn't a dream of his. It was real!

There it was again, filling the night with mournfulness, and yet with beauty too – what a strange, strange sound to hear up on the lonely hillside.

'What is it?' whispered Colin at last.

'Don't you know?' said Peter. 'It's someone playing a violin! That's all it is. But oh, what wonderful playing! No tune. Just playing like the wind plays, or the trees, going on and on and on!'

'A violin!' said George. 'Of course! But I've never heard one played quite like that before. Who's playing it? And why, out on this hill in the dark night?'

Then they heard Matt's voice, stern and clear in the darkness.

'Who are you? Come forth and show yourself!'

The sounds stopped at once, and not another note was heard. Matt stood at his door for a few minutes and then went inside his hut. The boys heard the door shut.

'Sit down here,' said Peter, in a low, excited voice. 'I want to say something.' They all sat down, and in the darkness Peter spoke urgently.

'That violin! It must be the one that was stolen! I've never heard a violin played like that before – the notes were so pure and so lovely. And to think that Matt called it wailing!'

'Well – it *was* a kind of wailing – violin music often does wail,' said Colin. 'But it was beautiful. Yes – I bet it was the stolen violin. But who was playing it?'

'Luke Bolan!' said Peter promptly.

'How do you know?' asked George.

'Well – we know he plays the banjo, so he may be able to play the violin too,' said Peter. 'And his banjo was burnt in the fire – so maybe he stole that violin to make up for it.'

There was a silence after this. Then Peter spoke again. 'The next thing for us to do is to find the violin – he probably hides it in his caravan,' he said. 'Let's go quietly over to it now, and see if there's a light inside. Better be very careful, because if Luke was playing it on the hillside, he may still be out there. No torches on, please!'

The three boys crept over towards the caravan. Would they see Luke inside, with the violin? The *stolen* violin?

CHAPTER SEVENTEEN

Where is the violin?

AT FIRST the three boys could not see the caravan at all, the night was so dark. They stumbled forward as quietly as they could, holding out their hands in front of them.

'Sh!' said Peter suddenly and stopped. The others bumped into him. 'Look!' whispered Peter. 'You can just see the outline of the caravan against the dark sky. Isn't that it?'

'Yes,' whispered back Colin. 'But there's no one there – it's quite dark.'

'Strange!' said Peter. 'Well – let's go as close as we can. Stop if you hear the slightest noise.'

They crept right up to the silent caravan. Not a chink of light was to be seen. Peter crept up the steps and listened. Ah – there *was* a sound inside! But what was it?

'It's someone crying!' said Colin. Yes – there was someone sobbing quietly, like a child!

'It must be little Benny, left all alone in the van,' said Peter. 'Is the pram anywhere about?' He switched on his torch to see. But it was not in its usual place beside the caravan, and was  nowhere to be seen. The sobbing still went on inside the van.

Then a voice made them jump almost out of their skins. It was old Matt again! He must have seen their torches and come over from his shack.

'Didn't I tell you lads to clear off home?' he said. 'Peter, does your father know you're out? And what are you doing on the steps of that caravan?'

'Matt – that wailing – it was someone playing a violin!' said Peter.

Matt stood silent a moment. Then he spoke in a voice of wonder. 'I think you're right! But I've never heard a fiddle played like that before. A-wailing and a-woe-ing! Who played it? There's no one in the Bolans' caravan, except young Benny tonight, that I do know for the Bolans asked me to keep an eye on it, while they went down to see someone about a cottage.'

'Oh – then it's poor little Benny crying in there because he's frightened of the wailing too!' said Peter. 'Shall we go in and comfort him?'

'No. He's afraid of people,' said the shepherd. 'But he's not afraid of old Matt! You let me see to him instead, Peter. I'll rock him to sleep like a weakly lamb! It's only that violin that's scared him. And that's a strange thing to be sure – someone up here making such mournful music at night!'

Matt walked into the dark caravan, making soft, comforting noises in his deep, kind voice. Peter flashed his torch swiftly inside, and saw Benny's dark head on a pillow in a corner. Old Matt bent over him.

The boys left the caravan in silence, and

began to walk home. They were filled with curiosity and were extremely puzzled.

Peter spoke first. 'I don't understand all this. It *must* have been Luke playing that violin somewhere on the hillside. But why? Matt seems quite certain that he and Mrs Bolan went off to the town, and left Benny in the van. They took the baby with them, of course, as the pram is gone. Well, then – why did Luke Bolan apparently come back, all on his own, and play a violin?'

'I don't know,' said Colin. 'But I'm perfectly certain in my own mind that it was Luke who stole that violin, and uses it to comfort himself with because his banjo has been burnt. He may have left his wife down in the town for an hour or two, and come up here to play it.'

'Well – where do you suppose he hides it?' asked George. 'He must hide it very carefully somewhere – because if it were found he'd go to prison for theft!'

'He probably hides it in his caravan, under the mattress – or in the bread-bin, or some such place,' said Peter. 'I think we ought to come up tomorrow and see if we can find it. Luke will be off to some fair or other, earning his living, and we know Mrs Bolan takes the baby and Benny to go shopping. Janet and I met her in the town the other morning.'

'All right. We'll come up here tomorrow,' said George. 'I feel as if I MUST get to the bottom of this. It's all so strange – the fire – the missing scarecrow clothes – the stolen violin – the wailing in the night – and yet no one about to play the violin!'

'Look out!' hissed Colin suddenly, and the three stopped walking very suddenly. A figure stood not far off, still and silent in the big field. Peter chuckled.

'Idiot! It's our old friend the scarecrow! I'm glad to see he's still wearing his new clothes. Come on – we shall all get into awful rows if we're much later!'

'What time shall we meet tomorrow?' asked George. 'Shall we all go – the whole Secret Seven? We'll take something up to the Bolans as an excuse for calling.'

'Right. As near ten o'clock as you can manage,' said Peter. 'Then we can get back in good time for lunch.'

They parted at Peter's front gate and went to their homes, thinking over the night's adventure

– for it really had been an adventure! All except that silly business when Susie and Binkie tried to upset everything!

'I hope to goodness they don't get to hear that we're going up to the caravan tomorrow,' thought George as he went home. 'Jack really ought to be more careful. He deserves to be chucked out of the Secret Seven if he can't keep Susie and her giggling friend in order!'

Jack somehow managed to keep Susie in complete ignorance of what was happening, and arrived at Peter's in good time the next morning. Everyone was there. A very brief meeting was held, at which Peter explained to the girls and to Jack exactly what had happened the night before. They listened in astonishment and envy, especially poor old Jack, who had had to escort Susie and Binkie home!

'Gosh – to think it was someone playing a *violin*!' said Jack. 'I wish I'd heard it. Bother Susie! I bet it was Luke Bolan playing it! Well – what a bad lot he is – smashing a window to steal a really valuable old violin!'

'Come on,' said Peter, standing up. 'Yes, you too, Scamper. Mother's given us some butter and biscuits to take up to Mrs Bolan, so they will make a nice excuse for seeing her, if she happens to be there. If she isn't we shall have a chance to look inside the van to see if the violin is tucked away somewhere.'

Off they all went, Scamper running beside them, his tongue hanging out. Where were the Secret Seven off to now? Scamper didn't care if they were going to the moon, so long as he could go with them!

CHAPTER EIGHTEEN

An unexpected find

THE SEVEN arrived at Matt's hut and looked inside it. The shepherd was not there – in fact, they could see him a long way off, rounding up sheep on the opposite hill. He waved to them and they waved back. His dog was with him, working hard.

'Now to see if the Bolans' van is empty,' said

Peter, and they went across to it, carrying the biscuits and the butter. Scamper trotted on in front, his long tail waving happily to and fro.

'Mrs Bolan! Are you there?' called Peter. There was no answer at all.

'The pram's not here,' said Janet, sorry that she wouldn't see the dear little baby.

'Is the door locked?' asked Peter anxiously. 'I hope to goodness it isn't.' He ran up the steps and knocked. 'Mrs Bolan! Are you in?'

There was no answer. He pushed gently at the door, and it yielded, opening a little.

'I'll just put the butter and biscuits on the shelf!' he called to the others, and went right inside. The caravan smelt musty and rather unpleasant, and was not very tidy. The big mattress still lay on the floor, as if Mrs Bolan had left in a hurry and hadn't troubled to tidy anything. Even the dirty breakfast cups and plates were still left on the shelf.

'Can we come in too?' called Janet.

'No. I'll just have a quick hunt round myself, and then one of you can come in, and check round to see that I haven't missed any hiding-place,' said Peter. 'We'd get in each other's way if we all came in, it's so small. It shouldn't be difficult to find a violin hidden here.'

The others stood outside, some on the caravan steps, some on the grass, peering in to see what Peter was doing. He searched very thoroughly indeed.

'Nothing under or in the mattress!' he called. 'Nothing in the cupboard. Wait, there's a shelf almost in the roof of the caravan – there's a long box there – that might be it!'

He took down the box and opened it – but it was quite empty except for a few mildewed papers that might even have belonged to Matt, when *he* had the caravan!

Peter searched everywhere. Then he came to the door, rather disappointed. 'No go!' he said. 'The violin is definitely not here. I suppose it might be hidden under a bush somewhere – but I don't think so, because that would ruin it – even if it had a case, which it hasn't. The case was left behind in the shop. Janet – you come up and search.'

Janet leapt up the steps, and the others watched her searching too. Peter told Colin and Jack to look *under* the caravan as well, for there were a few things there. But no – the violin

was certainly not among them. It was very, very disappointing.

Then suddenly Janet gave a loud squeal, and made everyone jump. 'What is it?' they cried.

'Look what I've found hanging behind the caravan door!' she cried. 'It was opened flat against the wall, and I didn't think of looking behind it till this moment. LOOK!'

And she displayed something very, very

surprising to the rest of the Seven. Not the stolen violin – but the stolen scarecrow clothes!

Yes, there they were – the old tweed coat, the dirty hat, and grey flannel trousers!

Everyone stared in amazement, recognising the clothes at once.

'But – but – how did they come to be in the caravan?' said Janet.

'Easy! Luke stole them from the scarecrow, wore them as a disguise to steal the violin, then came back to the van and hung them behind the door!' said Jack. 'Who would bother about old clothes in a van? No one would know they once belonged to a scarecrow!'

'Oh dear!' said Pam. 'I can't help feeling awfully sorry for poor Mrs Bolan. I'm sure she didn't know Luke stole the scarecrow clothes – or the violin. Where *can* that violin be? It simply *must* be hidden somewhere!'

'Well, it's certainly not here,' said Peter. 'And as I'm sure it's not hidden in the bushes, there's only one place I can think of!'

'Where's that?' asked the others, eagerly.

'In the baby's pram,' said Peter. 'No one would ever think anything was hidden in such a place, certainly not a valuable violin. I bet that's where it's kept.'

'But, Peter – it would ruin a violin to be bounced about on all day – and the baby is a very bouncy one!' said Pam.

'It could easily be wrapped round and round in some thick material,' said Peter. 'Easily! I bet I'm right!'

'Well – what do we do *now*, then?' asked Colin. 'We *think* Luke stole the scarecrow clothes to disguise himself – we *think* he stole that violin because his banjo was burnt – we *think* he plays it out on the hills at night – and now we *think* it's hidden in the baby's pram. But we can't prove a single thing!'

'If we could only look inside the pram, we should know,' said Jack.

'But how can we do that?' asked Peter.

'Sh!' said Jack suddenly. 'Look who's coming!'

They turned in a hurry – and saw Mrs Bolan hurrying along with the baby in the pram. It was howling loudly. Benny ran by his mother's side, holding on to the pram.

At first Mrs Bolan didn't see the children beside the caravan. Peter shut the door hurriedly, and then they all went towards her, hardly knowing what to say.

'There, there, little love,' she was saying to the baby. 'You're starving, aren't you, poor lamb!' She picked it up and turned to take it to the caravan, suddenly startled to see the seven children. She tried to smile her usual smile – but her face was worried and anxious, quite without its usual cheerful expression.

'Why, good morning, my dears,' she said. 'I'm just going to feed the baby. I've been down the town all the morning, and she's starving, poor mite. I meant to be back before this!'

She hurried into the caravan, and Benny went too.

'What about looking into the pram now?' said Pam, in a low voice. 'It's our only chance. Oh – I DO hope the violin isn't there!'

She bent over the pram and pulled away a dirty covering. Peter burrowed deep down into the wall of the pram, surprised to find his fingers trembling. He felt something long and hard, wrapped in thick cloth! He pulled it out.

He unwrapped a little of the cloth – and part of a violin handle showed at once! 'Yes – it *is* the violin!' said Peter, shocked. 'Now what do we do?'

CHAPTER NINETEEN

Little Benny

A LOUD voice made all the Secret Seven jump.
They looked up, to see a man walking up to
them – a tall, stooping fellow, with thick black
hair and eyes exactly like Benny's – Luke
Bolan. He looked very angry.

'You give me that! Poking and prying! I'll
box your ears, the lot of you!'

'Are you Luke Bolan?' said Peter. 'Well, isn't this the violin that was stolen from the antique shop?'

There was a scream from behind them, and Mrs Bolan came flying out of the caravan, Benny behind her.

'Luke! Luke! Leave those children be! Don't you dare harm them. Oh, look at that now – they've found the violin!' And to the children's utter dismay, she covered her face with her hands and began to sob. Benny began to sob, too, in fright, pulling at her dress.

Luke took the violin roughly from Peter, and held it up in the air as if he were going to dash it to the ground and break it. But Mrs Bolan held his arm at once.

'No, Luke, no. That would only make things worse. What do you children know about this? How did you find out?'

'It's too long a tale to tell,' said Peter. 'But Colin here actually saw your husband smash the window and take the violin – and he saw that he was wearing our old scarecrow's clothes: and I'm afraid we've just seen them hanging in your caravan. And now, of course, we've found the violin!'

'Oh, Luke, Luke, what have you done to us?' wept Mrs Bolan. 'You'll go to prison, sure as the sun is in the sky – and then what's to happen to me and the children? All our things burnt – and me left with the baby and poor little Benny!'

Luke put his arms round her, looking very sad indeed. Mrs Bolan flashed round on the children.

'I was going to put back that violin in the shop this very morning! Yes, that I was – and Luke here, he'll tell you the same. We didn't know it was so valuable! Luke thought it was so old-looking that it wasn't worth much!'

'I see,' said Peter, suddenly understanding. 'Of course – it does look very, very old. But didn't Luke see the notice beside it?'

'Yes,' said Luke. 'But that didn't mean anything to me.'

'Luke can't read,' said Mrs Bolan, wiping her eyes. 'He never went to school – he lived in a caravan all the time he was a child, and wasn't anywhere long enough to get schooling. If he'd have seen the notice and read how old and precious the violin was, he'd never have taken it – would you, Luke?'

'No, I wouldn't,' said Luke. 'I never thought it was worth more than a few pounds – and I'd not got even those, after our shack caught fire. I meant to go in and pay later. But I needed that violin so badly.'

'Why? Just because your banjo was burnt?' asked Colin, rather scornfully.

'Banjo? No, I didn't care so much about *that*!' said Luke, surprised. 'I can always borrow a banjo. No, young man, it was for my Benny I wanted the violin.'

'Benny! But – surely he can't play a violin!' cried Janet, amazed.

'Benny, love – do you want to give us a tune?' said Mrs Bolan, bending over the scared-looking little boy. He couldn't understand what was going on, and he was very frightened. Why was his mother crying?

Luke took the violin from the pram, where he had laid it when he went to comfort his wife. He put it into the eager little hands that went out for it – Benny's small brown hands, that seemed to come alive when they felt the smoothness of the old violin.

He walked a little way away, and stood with his back to them. He put the violin under his chin, and raised the bow – and on the air came once again that strange 'wailing', unearthly and beautiful, that the boys had heard the night before. No tune – just a series of beautiful sounds as if Benny was singing his own strange thoughts.

'He's playing to himself – just as the black-bird sings to himself, listening all the time,' thought Janet.

'No, no, Benny – play "The Dancing May-Tree!"' called his mother. 'Not your own tunes!'

And straightaway the boy swept into the merriest, lightest dance that the children had ever heard – joyous, breath-taking, astonishing. They gasped in wonder.

Mrs Bolan smiled round at them. 'There! That's an old gipsy tune. Benny plays them all! My little

Benny! You've never heard him play, have you? He . . .'

'Well – we did hear him last night, when it was dark,' said Peter. 'And old Matt heard him the night before. But he only played that kind of *wailing* music of his own, and Matt was puzzled and told us about it.'

'So we came up last night to see if we could hear it too – and we did,' said Colin. 'But we knew at once that it was someone playing a violin most beautifully. And we guessed the violin was a very good one – the stolen one, in fact!'

'Oh, Benny, Benny – and I left you asleep in bed!' said Mrs Bolan. 'And so I did the night before. You got out of bed, found the violin and took it out to play on the hillside – is that what you did?'

Benny didn't answer. He didn't even turn to face his mother. He was rubbing the bow gently on the strings, making a curious sound like the wind in the trees. Janet suddenly realised that that was exactly what he *was* playing – the actual little song that the wind was whispering in the nearby birch-tree!

'But he's a genius!' she thought. 'I hardly

129

know which is the violin and which is the wind.'
Then she spoke out loud.

'Mrs Bolan! Benny's wonderful! He's a
little genius! Oh, why don't you send him to
school? Why don't you let him be taught music
properly?'

'Benny wouldn't be any good at school,
Miss,' said Mrs Bolan, and she drew the child
to her. 'Why, surely you know what's the matter

with him? My Benny is blind.'

Blind! Now the children knew why those
great dark eyes had no expression in them, and
why Benny was so careful when he walked!
Poor, poor little Benny.

'Music is the only thing that keeps him
happy,' said Mrs Bolan. 'And when he lost his

own violin in the fire it seemed as if his heart was broken. That's why Luke took that old violin – just to make our little Benny happy again!'

CHAPTER TWENTY

Meeting of the Secret Nine!

THE SEVEN looked at Mrs Bolan, and then at the silent mysterious little Benny. Janet felt tears coming to her eyes. What could they do to help this gifted little boy? SOMETHING must be done! But the Secret Seven couldn't do it. No, the grown-ups must come into this – they always knew what to do!

And so it was that the Seven went to Peter's father and mother that morning, and poured out the whole story to them.

'We don't know what to do now, Mother,' said Peter, when the tale was ended. 'The violin must go back to the shop – but, Daddy, poor Luke mustn't be put into prison! Benny must go to school, and he *must* be taught music – and he must have a violin of his own. The

Secret Seven are quite prepared to buy one for him, even if they have to save for a year.'

'You're a good set of kids,' said his father, pleased. 'This is a most remarkable story, I must say! I don't know how you Seven get mixed up in things of this sort! Now first, about the violin. We can quite well give it back without any harm coming to Luke. Matt tells me he's a good enough fellow – and I don't expect he would have stolen that violin if he hadn't been so upset at Benny's being burnt.'

'He simply loves Benny!' said Pam. 'But how can the violin be given back without Luke coming into it?'

'There's a reward offered for its return – and if returned in good condition, no questions will be asked,' said Peter's father. 'I proposed to take it back myself, and say that I can't explain how it came into my possession – but that the man who took it is very sorry – and naturally I could not take any reward. That should settle that.'

'Oh good!' said all the Secret Seven, and then Scamper thumped his tail on the floor.

'And what about Benny?' asked Janet.

'I think I can help there,' said her mother. 'He can go to one of the schools run for blind children, and his gift for music will be developed to the utmost. He won't mind so much leaving his mother if he can have his precious music, and he will have all his holidays with her, of course!'

'Oh, thank goodness!' said Barbara and Pam, together. It had been a terrible shock to the Seven to learn that little Benny, with his beautiful dark eyes, was blind. But now it wouldn't matter so much – he would always be happy with his music!

'Well – it isn't often the Secret Seven have a Secret *Nine* meeting!' said Peter's father, smiling. 'I must say that Mummy and I feel highly honoured, Peter. Grown-ups are quite a help sometimes, aren't they?'

'Oh, Daddy – we couldn't do without you!' cried Janet, and gave him a sudden hug. 'Do you *mind* taking the violin back to the shop? You're sure you won't be arrested?'

'Quite sure,' said her father. 'And what's more, if the Secret Seven really do mean to get money together to buy little Benny a violin, I'd like to help too – and so would Mummy, of

course. I could have a look at the violins in the music shop, and see if there's one that would suit a small boy – so that Benny won't fret for his own burnt one any more.'

'Oh YES!' cried all the Seven together, and Scamper thumped his tail once more. He had no idea what was going on, but he was certainly enjoying it all. What other dog in the world would be allowed in at an important secret meeting like this?

Peter's father lost no time in dealing with the violin. He never told the Seven exactly what had passed between him and the antique-shop dealer – he merely said that all was well, and that Luke's name had not been mentioned.

'But I shall have a word or two with Luke myself,' he said. 'Just to make sure that he knows he was *almost* in very serious trouble.'

'Have you got another violin for Benny?' asked Janet anxiously.

'You can go up to Mrs Bolan and tell her to take Benny down to the music shop tomorrow, and they will let him try their smaller ones,' said Daddy. 'And then bring her here for Mummy to talk to her about school for Benny. Dear me, we do seem to be meddling in other people's affairs!'

'Not meddling – just giving a helping hand!' said his wife. 'As for the Secret Seven, Peter, you'll have to keep them all up to the mark, you know – and help to pay for Benny's violin!'

The Seven kept their word, of course. They had never in their lives been so busy earning money in holiday time! They found themselves jobs of all kinds, and even Susie joined in!

'Binkie's gone home, thank goodness,' said Jack. 'So Susie is just a bit more sensible. Mother says we're to allow her to get a job and give us the money if she wants to. She says it will do Susie good.'

'Oh well – if it's possible to do Susie good by all means let her work hard!' said Peter. 'But all the same, she is NOT going to come to our next Secret Seven meeting.'

When the day of the meeting came, two days before they went back to school, what a pile of money they had to count – plenty to buy the violin that Benny was already very, very happy with! He was to take it to the blind school with him, and that pleased him very much.

'Well – you've all worked very hard,' said Peter, looking round at the Seven. 'It's been rather exciting, hasn't it? Thanks for all your money, Secret Seven. Oh, and here's a bit more.' He emptied several coins on to the upturned box in front of him.

'Who's that from? Susie?' asked George.

'No. It's from Scamper!' answered Peter, with a laugh. 'He gave up two large bones and one little one in order to help Benny – and here's his money! Thanks most awfully, Scamper! You're a brick!'

'Wuff!' said Scamper happily. 'Wuff-wuff-wuff-wuff-wuff!'

'He says it's a pleasure to help us!' said Peter solemnly. 'And he really *does* like the Secret Seven!'

So do we, Peter. So do we!

SECRET SEVEN FIREWORKS

Contents

1 What's happened to the Secret Seven? 143

2 Password, please! 150

3 Plenty of plans 157

4 Saturday morning 164

5 A Nasty-looking lot 170

6 The bonfire is begun 177

7 Colin has some news 183

8 Another meeting 190

9 Susie really is annoying 196

10 A wonderful guy 203

11 One up to the tiresome three 210

12 Jack can be tiresome too! 217

13 Face at the window 224

14 A dreadful shock 231

15 Oh, that tiresome three! 238

16 Keep guard on the bonfire! 246

17 A space – and a button! 252

18 Jack has a sudden idea 258

19 Quote a lot happens 264

20 Bank! Crash! Whoosh! 272

CHAPTER ONE

What's happened to the Secret Seven?

PETER, JACK and Janet were walking home from school one fine October day, when someone came skipping up behind them. It was Susie, Jack's sister.

'Hallo, you three!' she said. 'What's happening to the Secret Seven? You never seem to have meetings now.'

143

'Nothing's happened to the Secret Seven,' said Peter. 'Don't be silly.'

Susie began to chant a little song just behind them.

> 'The Secret Seven's falling to bits.
> It doesn't meet any more.
> The only thing that is left of it
> Is the silly S.S. on the door!'

'*Susie!* You little horror!' said Jack, angrily. 'Singing like that in the street about the Secret Seven! Falling to bits! You don't know what you're talking about.'

'Oh, I *do*,' said Susie, skipping in front of them now. 'I know you haven't met for ages – I know. Jack's lost his badge – I know you can't use Peter's shed for meeting-places – I know . . .'

Peter, Janet and Jack glared at the smiling, irritating Susie.

'What do you mean – you know we can't use our shed?' demanded Peter. 'You've been snooping.'

'No, I haven't. My ball went over your wall, Peter, and I ran to get it – and I saw your shed full of onions! *Onions!*' Susie laughed loudly. 'So I knew you couldn't be meeting there – and I've a very particular reason for asking if the Secret Seven is still going on or not.'

Peter stopped at once, and the others stopped too. *Now* what was Susie up to? Why was she so anxious to know about the Secret Seven?

'What's this silly, particular reason?' asked Peter, sharply. 'Go on – tell us.'

'Well, you see – if your Secret Seven has stopped, I thought *I'd* like to form a Secret Seven Club of my own,' said Susie, solemnly, with a wicked glint in her bright eyes. 'I thought I'd ask Leonard, and Harry and . . .'

'What! Copy *us*!' said Janet, in scorn. 'Well – *I* wouldn't want to be a copy-cat like that!'

'And anyway, forget about it,' said Peter. 'The Secret Seven is meeting this very Saturday morning. Isn't it, Jack?'

This was the first that Jack had heard of any meeting but he nodded his head vigorously. 'Yes. Let me see – ten o'clock, wasn't it, Peter?'

'That's right,' said Peter, giving Janet a little

nudge in case she should say *she* hadn't heard of any meeting.

'It'll be a pretty smelly meeting, sitting on top of all those onions,' said Susie. 'Shall I help you to clear them out of the shed?'

'*No!*' roared Peter and Jack together.

Janet gave Susie a push. 'Go away!' she said, fiercely. 'You're just *trying* to be annoying. Fancy thinking *you* could run a club!'

'I could, easily,' said Susie. 'You just wait and see!'

She skipped off, leaving the other three feeling really furious. 'Can't you possibly keep that sister of yours in order, Jack?' said Peter. 'Like I do Janet?'

'You do *not* keep me in order,' said Janet, at once, and stalked off ahead of the two boys. They looked at one another.

'*Girls!*' said Jack, in a disgusted voice, low enough for Janet not to hear. 'They're all the same.'

'Except that Susie is a bit worse,' said Peter. 'Now look, Jack, we'd better have this Secret Seven meeting, as we've said we're going to. It's an awful bore, really, because we'll have to turn all those onions out and put them somewhere else. I hope my father won't mind!'

'Well, look, let's all come at a quarter to ten, not ten, and help you,' said Jack. 'We can easily tell the others in good time.'

'All right,' said Peter. 'Quarter to ten, then – and tell Susie if she dares to so much as put her nose round the door of our shed, I'll . . . I'll – well, I really can't think of anything bad enough to do to her.'

'What shall we have a meeting about?' said Jack. 'Nothing much has happened – no mystery or anything to work on. But we must have something to *talk* about.'

'Well, we will,' said Peter, an idea suddenly coming into his head. 'What about planning for Bonfire Night? It will be here in a couple of weeks or so, and we ought to start saving up for fireworks. Dad will take us to the shops when we have enough money.'

'Gosh, yes!' said Jack, thrilled. 'Of course – that's what we'll have the meeting about. We ought to decide about a guy and where to have our bonfire. Jolly good idea of yours, Peter.'

'And for goodness' sake find your badge,' said Peter. 'Susie said you'd lost it.'

'What a tell-tale!' said Jack. 'I *had* lost it. It went to the cleaner's on the lapel of my blazer – Mother didn't notice it. And I was awfully upset when the blazer came back without it, and grumbled like anything. That's how Susie knew it was gone.'

'Well, you'd better get your mother to make you a new one,' said Peter. 'Can't have anyone turning up without a badge, you know.'

'All right, all right. Why don't you lose *yours*

for once?' said Jack. 'Then you'd know what it feels like. How was *I* to know that my mother was going to send my blazer to the cleaner's all of a sudden?'

Peter gave him a friendly punch. 'Don't be so touchy! Tell George about the meeting on Saturday, will you? And I'll tell Colin. Janet will tell Pam and Barbara.'

'Right,' said Jack, as Peter swung in at the gate. 'There's one good thing to be said for Susie – she's made us call a meeting! I shall look forward to it. So long, Peter!'

'So long!' said Peter, and ran down the path that led to the shed where the Secret Seven met. He opened the door – and a dozen onions rolled out at once. He kicked them back.

'You wait till Saturday!' he said. 'You'll have to get out of here, and make room for the Secret Seven! Janet – Janet! Where are you? Gosh – won't it be fun to have one of our meetings again!'

CHAPTER TWO

Password, please!

ON SATURDAY morning Janet and Peter were down by their shed, together with two or three barrows of all sizes, ready to wheel away the onions stored there. The gardener hadn't been at all pleased when he heard that his precious onions were to be taken out of the nice dry shed.

'But we asked Dad, and he *said* we could put them into the old summer-house,' said Peter.

'Rain blows in there,' said the gardener.

'Dad said we could take the old tarpaulin sheet and cover them over with that,' said Janet. 'You see this really *is* our shed. We meet here. You know we do.'

'Not for weeks you haven't,' said the

gardener. 'Well, I'm busy – you'll have to move the lot yourselves. Take you a good time, too!'

'Oh, there'll be seven of us,' said Peter. 'Many hands make light work, you know.'

'You be careful that too many cooks don't spoil the broth,' said the man, and walked off, his rake over his shoulder.

'That was quite a bright answer,' said Janet, astonished. 'We'll have to tell the others that. Now let's see – three barrows; and look, wouldn't it be easier to *shovel* up the onions, instead of picking them up in two and threes as we said?'

'Now *you're* quite bright!' said Peter. 'I'll go to the tool shed and see what I can find. Hope the gardener's not there. He's a bit gloomy this morning. If the others come, ask them the password and see they've got their badges on.'

Janet began to put the onions into one of the barrows. She had put in about twenty when Colin and George came along.

'Hallo!' said Janet. 'Password, please.'

'It's so long since we had a meeting that we've forgotten it,' said Colin. 'Anyway, we'll hear it when the others come. It's only when we enter the shed that we have to say it. Do *you* know it, Janet?'

'Yes,' said Janet. 'But I had to look it up in my diary. I'd better not tell you it, in case Peter is cross. Come on – help me with the onions. Oh, wait a minute. Have you got your badges on? Good! Peter told me to look and see.'

'This sounds quite like old times,' said Colin. 'We oughtn't to have gone so long without a meeting.' He began to scoop up onions in his hands.

'Here are Pam and Barbara,' said Janet, hearing footsteps. 'Hallo, you two! Password, please!'

Colin and George pricked up their ears at once. Aha – now they would know it!

'Wee Willie Winkie,' said the two girls together, and Janet nodded. 'That's right,' she said. 'Er – password, boys?'

Colin and George repeated it solemnly, and Pam giggled. 'You'd forgotten it,' she said. 'Gosh – what a lot of onions.'

Peter came back at that moment with Scamper at his heels. He carried one big spade and two small ones.

'Password!' said George, pointing at him. 'And it's *not* Jack the Giant-Killer!'

'Quite right. It's Wee Willie Winkie!' said Peter, with a grin. 'Isn't it, Scamper?'

'Wuff,' said Scamper, pleased to see so many people.

'Let's see – Jack's not come yet,' said Peter. 'Ah – here he is. Has he got his badge on? He said it had gone to the cleaner's on his blazer, and hadn't come back. I told him he'd have to ask his mother to make him another.'

'Hallo, hallo!' said Jack, coming up at a run.

'Am I last? Sorry – but I quite forgot that I'd lost my badge. I went to ask Mother to make one and . . .'

'But that looks like your *old* one on your coat,' said Janet. 'A bit scruffy!'

'It *is* my old one,' said Jack. 'And what's more Susie found it for me! She said that when cleaners find brooches or badges or anything like that on clothes sent to be cleaned, they pop them into an envelope and put them in a pocket. And Susie looked in the breast pocket of my blazer, and there was my badge, inside a little envelope. I'd have been awfully late if she hadn't found it.'

'Well! Fancy *Susie* doing you a good turn!' said George, astonished. 'Good for *her*! We're all here now – let's hurry up and move all these onions and get on with the meeting.'

It didn't take long for the seven of them to shovel up the onions into three barrows and wheel them away to the summer-house. Soon they were all neatly piled there and Peter and Jack pulled the old tarpaulin over them to keep them dry.

'Now we'll go back to the shed and hold our

meeting,' said Peter. 'We'll get a few boxes to sit on, and after the meeting we'll clear up the shed and make it neat and tidy again.'

Back they all went to the shed. Peter was surprised to see that the door was now shut, and even more surprised to find Scamper there, growling at it! What *was* the matter with him?

Peter tried to open the door. It was locked from inside! A familiar voice came from the shed, with an aggravating little giggle at the end of it.

'Password, please!'

'*Susie!*' yelled everyone, and Peter shook the door angrily.

'Susie, how dare you? This is *our* meeting-place. Open the door at once.'

'In a minute. I just wanted to sit here and think what a horrible shed this is,' said Susie. 'Pooh! It smells! Now, when I have *my* club, I shan't meet in an onion shed, I shall meet in a . . .'

'Susie! *Will* you open the door?' yelled Peter, banging on it furiously.

'On one condition,' said Susie. 'And that is that you let me walk out without speaking to me or touching me. Otherwise I shall sit here all morning and hold a Secret Seven meeting by myself.'

Peter knew when he was beaten. 'All right, you idiot. Come on out. We want to hold our meeting before the morning's gone. But we'll pay you back for this!'

The door opened and Susie sauntered out, grinning all over her cheeky face. Nobody said a word, though everyone longed to shout at her. She disappeared up the garden path, Scamper giving a few small, rather astonished barks.

'Good riddance to bad rubbish!' said Pam. 'Come on – do let's begin our meeting. Well – I'm glad Susie's not in the Secret Seven. *What* a nuisance she'd be!'

CHAPTER THREE

Plenty of plans

THE SEVEN trooped into the shed and looked
round. 'Better get a few boxes, as you said,
Peter,' said Janet. 'Pam, you come with me – I
know where there are some. You boys sweep
out the shed a bit. It's messy with onion
skins.'

Before long all the Seven, with Scamper
thumping his tail happily on the ground, were
seated on boxes round the shed. They felt quite

tired after all their shovelling and wheeling of barrows!

'Now, we've met to discuss plans for Bonfire Night,' said Peter, in a business-like way. 'It's still some time ahead, but it takes a good while to save up money for fireworks. Also we'll have to discuss a guy.'

'I vote we make a guy *exactly* like Susie,' said Pam. 'Awful girl!'

'No. Susie would simply *love* that,' said Jack, at once. 'She'd go round boasting about it. I vote we make a nice *big* guy – one that would look fine on top of a bonfire.'

'Oh yes – and let's have a *huge* bonfire!' said Barbara. 'The biggest we've ever made. We made a pretty big one last year, but I'd like a most enormous one. I love to see the flames blaze high!'

'Right. We'll have a great big bonfire – and a guy to match,' said Peter. 'That means we'll have to begin collecting stuff for it at once. It takes ages to build a big pile of burnable stuff.'

'Where shall we have it?' asked Colin.

'In my garden,' said Barbara. 'Then the next door kids could see it.'

'No. It's too far for us all to bring wood there,' said Peter. 'Actually I think it would be a good idea to have it in the big field just at the bottom of our garden here – for one thing there's a lot of dead wood in the hedges and in the little wood nearby, and it wouldn't be very far to carry it.'

'Yes. That's a good idea,' said Jack. 'We could have a simply enormous one out there in the field. We could meet in the wood, and collect dead twigs and branches together – that would be more fun than getting it on our own and dragging it here.'

'Right. That's settled then,' said Peter. 'We're getting on. Now about saving up for fireworks.'

'We'll all bring what we can, as we usually do,' said Barbara. 'I've got a bit of money in my savings box already that I can bring. Who shall be treasurer?'

'Better vote for one,' said Peter. He took out his notebook and tore a page from it. He then tore the page into seven neat strips, and handed a strip to each person. 'Everyone got a pencil?' he said. 'You haven't, Pam – well, take mine for a minute. Now – write down the person you think would be a good treasurer – someone to hold the money for us, and keep it safe, and count it each time we bring any. They'll have to keep the figures in a book, so that we know what we've got, and who brought it. Ready? Write the name down then of the one you want. It must be someone good at figures, of course. We don't want a muddle made of our money.'

They all sucked or chewed their pencils and frowned. A good treasurer? One who could manage figures well? One who wouldn't make a muddle?

They each scribbled a name on their piece of paper, folded it and handed it in to Peter. He unfolded each one – and then grinned.

'Hm – well!' he said. 'You all seem to think *I'm* the one – six votes for me! Thanks awfully.'

'But there are seven of us!' said Pam, surprised. 'Who didn't vote for you?'

'*I* didn't vote for myself, silly!' said Peter. 'Actually I voted for Jack. Well, that's settled. We'll meet here in the shed each Saturday at ten o'clock – unless we make different plans. Bring any firework money you have then. And when it's all written down in our fireworks book, we'll go off into the field and the wood and collect stuff for the bonfire.'

'Good,' said George, pleased. 'It's fun to be doing something again. We oughtn't to let so much time go by without a meeting.'

'What about a guy?' asked Colin. 'Who's going to see about him?'

'I think the three girls had better make a big, stuffed body,' said Peter. 'They are more likely to get stuff for the guy than we are. And they can sew better than we can.'

'Goodness – you can't sew at *all*!' said Janet. 'I've just thought of something. Mother said that old eiderdown off your bed was no good now – it's got the moth in. We could use that for the body – all nicely squashed up.'

'Oh *yes*,' said Barbara. 'That's a very good idea. And I believe we've got a dirty old rug somewhere in the loft at home too – that would help to make a good fat body!'

'Well, you girls have got some good ideas,' said Peter. 'We'll decide about clothes at another meeting. We'd better see the size of the guy's body before we try to fit him out with clothes.'

'Don't make him *too* enormous,' said Jack. 'Else we shan't be able to get old clothes to fit him!'

'Well – I think it's time we brought this very interesting meeting to an end,' said Peter. 'What about sweeping out this shed, and getting that old table we had, and putting up a shelf again?'

'Yes. We'll do that,' said Colin, getting up. 'Oh sorry, Scamper – did I tread on your tail? Hallo – who's this coming? If it's Susie, let's all chase her up the path!'

But it wasn't Susie. It was Peter's mother, carrying a tray of lemonade and biscuits.

'I don't know the password!' she said. 'But please let me in. If I say "Lemonade and biscuits!" will that do?'

'Oh, Mother – you *are* brilliant!' said Peter, in delight. He opened the door. 'Come in – we're all here – and we've had a *marvellous* meeting, and made all kinds of plans!'

'Well, it's nice to see the Secret Seven together again,' said his mother, setting down the tray on a box. 'There now – there are a few dog biscuits for Scamper, because I know he doesn't like being left out.'

'Wuff-wuff!' said Scamper, gratefully, and licked her hand.

Everyone settled down to eat and drink. They felt very happy. They had made plans – good ones too – and they could all work together once more, and meet each week – perhaps oftener.

'Well – here's to Bonfire Night!' said Peter, lifting up his glass. 'And a Great Big Guy!'

CHAPTER FOUR

Saturday morning

THE NEXT Saturday morning all the Seven met again. 'Wee Willie Winkie!' said everyone, and passed quickly into the shed. Peter shot a sharp look at each of them – yes, they all had on their badges – good!

The shed looked very neat and tidy now, swept out, and with sand sprinkled all over the floor by Peter, except where an old rug lay, given by Pam's mother. Two shelves were up, and on them stood some plastic cups and a plate or two. There was also a tin of toffees, and a second tin in which were home-made biscuits made by Peter's mother.

Scamper went to sit under the biscuit shelf,

looking up longingly, giving little whines every now and again.

'No, Scamper – it's not biscuit-time yet,' said Peter. 'Don't take any notice of him, anyone. He's had a good breakfast already. Scamper, be quiet.'

'I've got a report to make on the guy,' said Pam, importantly. 'He's coming along nicely.'

'Fine,' said Peter. 'Tell us about him.'

'Well, we took Barbara's old rug,' said Pam, 'and Janet's old eiderdown – goodness, it *was* moth-eaten! It's a good thing it's going to be burnt.'

'And we did a bit of rolling up and shaping,' said Janet, 'and really, it's not a bad body at all. Would you like to see it? It's just behind the shed, covered over with an old rubber sheet.'

'You shouldn't leave it there,' said Jack. 'Susie might get it.'

Janet went to fetch the guy's body. It certainly was quite fat, and the girls had really managed to shape it very well. It had a round head, a plump body, with a rope tied round it for a waist, and plump arms and legs.

'We haven't made the feet and hands yet!' said Janet. 'It's not bad, is it?'

Scamper was amazed to see such a curious-looking creature. He barked frantically, and seemed quite scared of it. The children laughed at him.

'Wait till it's all dressed up, Scamper,' said Janet. 'You'll bark all right then!'

'If any of us have old clothes that will fit this big fellow, please bring them to our next meeting,' said Peter. 'Or give them to Janet before that, if you can.'

'The guy had better be kept in here, hadn't it?' said Jack. 'If Susie comes snooping round, she *might* find it outside – and she's still thinking of making a club of her own, you know. If she does, they're sure to make a raid on the shed!'

'All right, we'll leave it here – right at the back, in its rubber sheet,' said Janet. 'I'm glad you all approve of it. Please don't forget to look out some nice big clothes – and a big hat or cap. We shall put a mask on him, and he'll look really fine.'

'Now about money,' said Peter. 'Anyone brought any?'

To everyone's delight, the money poured in! Fifty pence from Pam, a pound from Barbara, eighty pence from Colin, ninety pence from George, thirty pence from Jack, and two pounds between Peter and Janet.

'Five pounds fifty already,' said Peter, writing down names and money quickly, and adding it up. 'Pretty good.'

'Sorry about my thirty pence,' said Jack. 'But my gran had a birthday this week, and I spent most of my money on a present. I'll bring more next week. Dad has promised me fifty pence if I'll clean up the garage for him. I'll bring that.'

'That's all right,' said Peter. 'We've made a jolly good start. Now, what about a biscuit or two, and then we'll set off to look for dead wood for our bonfire.'

'Wuff!' said Scamper, at once, thumping his tail on the ground.

Everyone laughed.

'I don't know whether you deserve a biscuit, Scamper,' said Peter. 'You haven't brought in any money – you didn't help with the guy, and . . .'

'Wuff-wuff-wuff!' said Scamper, running over to Peter and putting a paw on his knee.

'He says, can he have a biscuit if he goes and picks up dead wood with us,' said Peter, solemnly. 'Shall we let him?'

'Yes!' shouted everyone, and Scamper received the very first biscuit out of the tin. Everyone took one, and then, locking the shed behind them, they set off, munching their own biscuits, to the field behind Peter's garden.

'Let's choose a place for the bonfire,' said Peter. 'Not too near the hedge, in case it gets burnt.'

'Just here then,' said Jack, walking to a nice flat patch. 'It's well away from the hedge, and we can all dance round it with plenty of room to spare, and let off fireworks.'

Everyone agreed, and Peter nodded. 'Another thing settled,' he said. 'Hallo, look – there's the man who cuts Dad's hedges and clears out the ditches. He might let us have all the trimmings to burn!'

An old fellow was standing a little way up the hedge, slashing at it with a sharp-edged tool. He was cutting away the untidy new growth made that year, and was shaping the hedge skilfully. The children went to him and watched him, admiring the way he cut and trimmed.

'Good morning, Mr Burton,' said Peter. 'You're making a very good job of that. Do you like hedging and ditching? You've cleared out the ditch well.'

'I like any job that takes me outdoors,' said the old fellow. 'Sun and wind and rain, that's what I like.'

'Could we have the hedge trimmings, do you think?' asked Peter. 'For a bonfire on Guy Fawkes Night?'

'You are welcome to them,' said Mr Burton. 'I'll leave this little lot here for you. Take them any time.'

'Oh good,' said Peter. 'We'll do that. Come along, all of you. We'll be off to the wood now, and hope we'll find stacks of dead wood. We're going to have a really busy morning!'

And across the field they ran to the wood, Scamper barking joyfully. What were the Secret Seven up to now? Scamper would help them whatever it was!

CHAPTER FIVE

A nasty-looking lot

THE SEVEN shuffled through the dead leaves in the wood. Except for the evergreen trees, the wood seemed very bare, and full of light. Peter kicked at a fallen branch.

'Here's a nice bit of wood for our fire! Let's make it the beginning of our collection, and bring whatever we find to this spot here under this big tree. Jack and I have brought plenty of rope. We can tie the whole lot up here when we've collected it, and drag it home.'

'Good idea,' said Colin. 'Let's separate then and hunt in different directions.'

The wood was full of dead twigs and fallen branches. There had been a great gale three

weeks before, and a good deal of dead or rotten wood had been blown down. The children were delighted to see so much. Soon they each had quite big bundles.

'I'm going to put my lot down where we planned we would,' said Pam. 'I keep dropping bits now. I've got so much.'

'I'll do the same,' said Janet. 'Gosh, look at Jack over there. He's dragging along half a tree! That's a great find!'

It was fun in the wood, shuffling through the dead leaves, hunting for firewood. One by one the Seven dragged their finds through the trees to the place they had arranged, under the big tree. Soon quite a good pile was there – big twigs, little twigs, small branches, big ones –

and good gracious, here came Peter, Jack and Colin dragging a most enormous branch!

'We'll have to chop this one up smaller,' panted Peter. 'Gosh – we *are* getting on, aren't we?'

'Let's go to the hedger's old hut and sit down for a bit,' said Jack. 'I'm really quite puffed. I've got two packets of sweets to share out. Let's go and sit down and eat them.'

'Good idea,' said Peter, and the Seven set off to Mr Burton's little hut, where he often had his dinner on a rainy day. It was just inside the wood, overgrown with brambles and ivy, and in the summer-time it was so green with the leaves that it could hardly be seen.

'I haven't been here before,' said Pam, as they came near to the hut. 'It must be nice to have a little hut all your own like this. I suppose Mr Burton won't mind us sitting in it, will he?'

'Oh no. Janet and I have often been inside,' said Peter.

Scamper suddenly began to bark as they came near the hut. Peter looked at him in surprise. 'What's the matter, old thing? There's nobody about – not even a rabbit!'

The spaniel stood quite still, his silky nose pointing towards the shed. 'Wuff-wuff-WUFF!' he barked.

'Can't be anyone here,' said Peter. 'Go and look, Scamper. You're just making a fuss.'

Scamper went slowly and stiffly over towards the shed, growling. Everyone watched, puzzled. He went right to the shed door, and then let off a loud volley of barks. An angry voice came from the shed.

'Clear off!' Then a stone came flying out, narrowly missing the surprised Scamper.

Peter raced up to the shed at once, and stood angrily at the door, glaring at three men inside. 'What do you mean by throwing stones at my dog? You nearly hit him. You might have lamed him.'

There came the sound of scornful laughter and then a stone came spinning out of the shed door and caught Peter on the ankle.

Scamper gave a fierce growl and darted forward. Peter just caught him in time before he went into the shed.

'You'd better get out of this shed,' cried the boy, angrily. 'It doesn't belong to you. It's

Mr Burton's hut. I'll fetch him over here to you if you don't clear out.'

He stood glaring at the three laughing men, and one of them sent another stone skimming through the door. It just missed Scamper. 'I'll go and get Mr Burton,' shouted Peter, and turned to go. He ran back to the others, who were all standing together, amazed.

'I'm going to get Mr Burton,' panted Peter. 'Watch and see if the men go.'

He shot off to find Mr Burton, but before he had time to come back, the three men came out of the shed, stood at the doorway a few seconds, and stared at the watching children. One of them shook his fist. The boys pushed the three girls behind them, as the men walked towards them. But they turned off between the trees, and disappeared, talking in low voices.

'What a nasty-looking lot,' said Janet, relieved to see them go. 'I wonder what they were up to in that shed?'

'Planning some kind of mischief, I should think,' said Colin. 'It would be a very good meeting-place for three rogues.'

'I've got a notebook,' said Jack. 'I'm going to jot down what the men are like – just in *case* it might be useful.'

'But how could it be?' said Pam.

'You never know,' said Jack. 'Hallo, here's Peter. Didn't you get Mr Burton?'

'No – he's gone off somewhere,' panted Peter. 'Those men gone?'

'Yes,' said Colin. 'And Jack's just going to

jot down some notes about them. We think they're probably plotting some kind of mischief. Let's see – one man was short and dark, and had a crooked nose . . .'

'Yes,' said Jack, writing. 'And one was big and fat, and had a moustache. No hat. Gingery hair.'

'And the third one was thin, and limped,' said Pam. 'His ears stuck out too. I noticed them.'

Jack finished scribbling and put his notebook away.

'Now let's take all our stuff back,' he said. 'Where are the ropes, Peter? Let's have the sweets in our own shed – I don't fancy Mr Burton's shed after those scruffy-looking men have been there!'

CHAPTER SIX

The bonfire is begun

PETER HAD three lengths of rope tied round his waist, and he now untied them and gave one each to Jack and George.

'Make a big bundle of wood and tie it with the rope,' he said. 'Come on, girls – you help me with my bundle!'

They were soon busy tying up the collected wood into enormous bundles. Then they put the ropes over their shoulders, and set off through the trees, pulling the bundles across the field to the place planned for their bonfire.

'This is fun,' said Janet, as she and Peter dragged one great bundle over the field. 'Oh, Pam – look, some of our bits have dropped out. You walk behind and pick them up for us.'

In about half an hour's time all the twigs and rotten branches were piled up well. The Seven stood back and looked at the heap proudly, Scamper wagging his tail as though he too had helped with the bundles! But all he had done was to carry one long twig back in his mouth, banging it against Peter's legs!

'There!' said Peter. 'That's a really good beginning, I must say. I tell you what, if anyone has half an hour to spare, I think they should pop along and collect a few more bits and pieces. Janet and I might be able to in our dinner-hour next week.'

'And I could race along from afternoon school perhaps, on my bike, at four o'clock sometime,' said George. 'It would still be light enough to hunt about.'

'Good,' said Peter. 'Every little helps, as my Dad says when he wants us to go weeding, and hopes we'll do half the garden!'

'Let's go and sit down and have Jack's sweets,' said Pam. 'I feel quite tired out.'

They left the pile of wood and went to sit in their own shed. Peter unlocked the door and they went in.

'I'm keeping the door locked because I've got our firework money in that box on the shelf,' he said. 'And also because of the guy. Susie just *might* come along and do something silly to it.'

'She wouldn't touch the money, though, you know that jolly well,' said Jack at once.

Peter nodded. 'Yes. I know that, of course. Come on – hand out the sweets, Jack. It's nearly dinner-time, but I bet they won't spoil our appetites. Not mine anyway, because we're having steak and kidney pudding, and *nothing* could put me off that.'

'*Why* did you have to mention steak and kidney?' groaned George. 'You've made me feel so hungry that I could eat all Jack's sweets at one go.'

Jack hastily stuffed the sweets back into his pocket. His hand touched his notebook, and he remembered that he had written the three men's descriptions in it. He drew it out, and read them out loud.

'It will be funny if we meet them again,' he said. 'We shall know where they're going – probably to Mr Burton's hut in the woods.'

'We shan't meet them again – not in Mr Burton's hut or anywhere else,' said Colin. 'They were just tramps, wandering over the country. They sat down for a rest in the hut, I expect.'

'Oh well – you never know,' said Jack, rather damped, and put his notebook back into his pocket. 'When's our next meeting, Peter?'

'Can you manage Thursday afternoon, after school?' said Peter. 'Not for finding wood, but just for seeing what guy clothes we get and if anyone has some more money. Then we shan't have to spend so much time on those things next Saturday morning; we can get straight on with collecting wood for the bonfire.'

'Right,' said Colin, and George and Jack nodded too.

'Pam and I may not be able to come,' said Barbara. 'We may have an extra dancing lesson then. We're in a concert soon, you know.'

'Well, come if you can,' said Peter. 'Same password – and badges, of course. There's our dinner-bell. We must go. See you on Monday, chaps!'

They all departed, and Peter and Janet and Scamper went up the path to their house.

'Wash your hands!' called their mother. 'My goodness me, you *are* dirty!'

'We've been collecting wood for our bonfire,' called back Janet. 'We won't be a minute.'

They told their mother all about their morning as they ate their steak and kidney pudding very hungrily indeed. When they came to the piece about the three men in the hut, their mother looked up sharply.

'Now listen – you are not to go into the wood unless there are at least three or four of you – certainly not alone. I don't like the sound of those men. There are some very bad men about in these days.'

'But, Mother, they were only tramps,' said Peter. 'And anyway, Scamper was with us.'

'Well, if you go into the wood you are to take Scamper with you,' said Mother. 'And you are not to let any of the girls wander about without you boys. Now that's an *order*. Do you understand, or shall I get Daddy to say so?'

'No – of course not. We'll do exactly what you say,' said Peter, surprised. 'Mother, you should just *see* our bonfire pile of wood – it's awfully big already.'

'I shall have to come and watch it when you set it alight,' said his mother. 'And see the fireworks too. By the way, Janet, if you want to earn firework money, you can do a little job for me.'

'Oh good. What, Mother?' asked Janet.

'You can turn out the linen cupboard and put back everything tidily for me,' said her mother. 'That will be a fifty pence job if you do it well.'

'Right, I'd love to,' said Janet. 'I like arranging things. I'll do it this very evening. Our next meeting is on Thursday, you know.'

But their next meeting came before Thursday after all. Something very exciting happened – and it was Colin who called the meeting, not Peter!

CHAPTER SEVEN

Colin has some news

ON MONDAY evening, when Peter and Janet were sitting quietly doing their homework, the telephone rang. Mother went to answer it.

She called to Peter. 'It's for you, Peter. Colin wants to speak to you. He sounds very excited.'

Peter shot to the telephone at once, and Janet went too. What had happened? Colin had walked part of the way home from school with Peter that afternoon, and hadn't seemed in the least excited about anything.

'Hallo? Peter here,' said Peter, and at once heard Colin's excited voice. 'Peter, can I come and see you *at once*? Something's happened. I want to call a meeting of the Secret Seven as soon as possible – tomorrow after school perhaps. Can I come right along now? I'll only be a minute or two on my bike.'

'Goodness – what's the matter?' said Peter, astonished. 'A meeting? Whatever about?'

'Can't tell you now. People might hear,' said Colin. This sounded very mysterious indeed.

'Well, come along at once,' said Peter. 'Better

come to the shed. We'll be alone there. See you soon.'

He put down the receiver, and stared at Janet, who was just beside him.

'What is it?' she said, excited.

'Don't know,' said Peter. 'He's coming in a few minutes – to the shed. He wants to call a meeting of the Secret Seven tomorrow. Whatever *can* be the matter?'

'I'm coming down to the shed too,' said Janet.

'No, you're not,' said Peter. 'All right, all right – don't look so fierce. I'll let you come, but remember, not a word to anyone unless I say so.'

'As if I *would* say anything!' said Janet, scornfully. 'Mother! Mother, where are you? Peter and I are going to slip down to our shed for a minute. Colin wants to see us about something important.'

'Aha! Secret Seven business, I suppose,' said her mother. 'All right, but put coats on, please. It will be cold down there tonight.'

They put on their coats and slipped down to the shed, with Scamper trotting happily at their heels. Peter unlocked the door, and lit a little oil-lamp his mother had given him for the shed. He set it carefully on a box.

The two waited patiently for Colin, trying in vain to think what could have excited him so. It must be something very important if he wanted to call a meeting! Any members had the

right to do this, though as a rule it was only Peter who did so.

Jingle-jingle! That was a bicycle bell. *Click* – that was the front gate. Then came the sound of footsteps as Colin hurried down the path to the shed, wheeling his bicycle.

He rapped at the door. 'Wee Willie Winkie,' he said, in a low voice, and Peter opened the door at once.

'What's all the excitement about?' Peter asked. 'Sit down and tell us.'

'I'll begin at the beginning,' said Colin,

whose face was red with cycling fast and with excitement. 'You know where my granny lives, don't you? Not far from my house, but round the corner?'

'Yes,' said Peter and Janet together.

'Well, she's away,' said Colin, 'but she's coming back tomorrow, so my mother asked me if I'd take some new-laid eggs to Granny's house – we keep hens, you know – and give them to Greta, her Austrian helper, so that Granny could have some poached eggs when she gets back. It's her favourite meal.'

He stopped and rubbed his hot face with his hanky.

'Go on,' said Peter. 'Do come to the point.'

'I *am*,' said Colin. 'Well, I took the eggs and ran up the road and round the corner. There was a light in the hall as usual – but I didn't knock at the front door, because I always go in the back way. It saves Greta coming to the door. Well, I slipped round the back way, and got to the kitchen door. It was shut, but not locked.'

'Wuff!' said Scamper, suddenly, and made them all jump.

'It's all right – he only saw a mouse run over the floor,' said Janet. 'Do go on.'

'I went inside,' said Colin. 'Greta wasn't in the kitchen, so I went through to the sitting-room. There was a light there, and I wondered if Granny had got back a day early. I pushed open the door – and my word *what* a mess I saw! Phew!'

'What kind of a mess?' asked Peter, thrilled.

'Everything upside down – drawers pulled out and emptied on the floor. The cupboard broken open. And then I saw Granny's safe – that was broken open too! She had it behind a big mirror – I didn't know that before. Someone had taken down the mirror, found the safe and smashed it open. It was empty!'

'*Colin!* How *awful*!' said Janet.

'Where was Greta?' said Peter. 'Surely *she* hadn't done all that!'

'Of *course* not,' said Colin. 'I suddenly heard a wailing noise, and rushed out into the hall. I traced the noise to the kitchen – and then to the larder, which was locked on the outside. I unlocked the door – and there was poor Greta inside, locked in!'

'What did you do next?' asked Peter, really excited.

'I telephoned the police,' said Colin. 'I felt frightfully important, ringing up the police-station. Two men came round at once – and by that time my mother and father were there too, because I phoned them as well.'

'But why do you want to call a meeting of the Secret Seven about this?' asked Peter. '*We* can't do anything.'

'Well, listen,' said Colin. 'I heard Greta giving details of the robbers to the police – three men – and she described two of them *exactly* as Jack described those men in his notebook – the men we saw. Greta didn't see the third – but I'm *sure* they must have been the men we saw in Mr Burton's hut – and for all we know they were planning the robbery then!'

'Whew!' said Peter. 'Think of that! Yes – we'll certainly call a meeting tomorrow. After afternoon school sharp at quarter past four. My word – what a thrill!'

CHAPTER EIGHT

Another meeting

TUESDAY SEEMED a very long day indeed to the Secret Seven. They longed for afternoon school to be over so that they could race off to the meeting-shed, and hear all that Colin had to say. He had actually been called out of school that morning by the police, who wanted to ask him questions!

'I bet he feels really important,' said Jack to Peter, as Colin walked out of the school-room. 'I'm longing for our meeting, aren't you?'

The meeting time came at last. Everyone was at the shed very punctually indeed, except Jack, who arrived last of all, panting for breath.

'Wee Willie Winkie,' he gasped. 'Sorry to be last, but it was Susie's fault. She wanted to know what was up, and when I wouldn't tell her, she went and hid my bike – and her own too – so I had to run all the way here on foot.'

'Sit down,' said Peter. 'Colin, begin your story, please.'

Colin told it all over again. He was sorry that it was his granny's house that had been robbed, but he couldn't help feeling very thrilled that he had been the one to discover the robbery, and telephone the police.

'So Greta saw two of the men, but not the third,' said Peter, when Colin had finished. 'Have you brought your notebook, Jack? I rather think we shall find the description of the third robber there!'

Jack fumbled for his notebook, his face alight with excitement. 'To think I wrote down all their descriptions – just by chance, really, because I happened to have my notebook!' he said. 'Wait a minute – yes, here are my notes. Colin, how did Greta describe the two men *she* saw?'

'She said one was very short and dark,' said Colin, 'and she specially noticed that his nose was crooked, and she said he had bad teeth.'

'Well, that answers exactly to my first description,' said Jack, excited. 'I've got "One man was short and dark, and had a crooked nose". I didn't notice his bad teeth.'

'The crooked nose is enough, really,' said Colin. 'Well, that was one man. Greta said the second man was thin, and had ears that stuck out from his head. She said she thought he was lame, but she wasn't sure about that.'

'Ha – she's right!' said Jack, looking at his notes again. 'Listen. I've got one man down as thin, and noted that he limped – well, that's Greta's second robber, no doubt about that! You say she didn't see the other one?'

'No – she said that the men burst in at the kitchen door, and she saw the first two quite clearly. The third man was behind them, so she couldn't describe him. The first two leapt at her, and she fell to the floor, poor Greta. They turned her on her face, and the third man bound her hands, and then they bundled her into the larder and locked the door. She wasn't really hurt – only scared stiff.'

'She must have been thrilled to see you when you opened the larder!' said Janet.

'She was! I undid her hands, and she put her arms round my neck and hugged me, and said hundreds of things in German, which I couldn't understand at all,' said Colin. 'Then she sat down, plump, on a chair – and *most* unluckily it was where I'd put the bag of eggs.'

Everyone roared with laugher, and then stopped, looking rather guilty.

'We oughtn't to have laughed,' said Janet. 'It's all very serious – but honestly – when I thought of poor Greta sitting down on Colin's eggs, I just couldn't help myself!'

'Well, Greta laughed too, when she found out,' said Colin. 'Actually she laughed and cried at the same time. Gosh. I did have a time – seeing to Greta, and telephoning the police and Mother and Dad – and waiting for the police to arrive – well, honestly, I half thought it must all be a dream!'

'I bet you did,' said Peter. 'Did you tell the police that you thought we'd seen the three men?'

'Yes, I did,' said Colin. 'But I didn't say anything about Jack writing down the descriptions of them, because I thought perhaps he'd like to tell them that himself. I mean – it might be an important clue.'

'Very decent of you,' said Jack. 'Shall we go to the police together, straight away now, Colin, with my notebook?'

'Yes, you'd better,' said Peter. 'They'll be interested to know we've got descriptions of the third man. Or rather, that you have, Jack. Good thing you wrote them down – you just *never* know when a thing like that is going to be useful.'

'I think we'll go now,' said Jack, getting up, looking rather important. 'Come on, Colin.'

'Thanks for calling the meeting, Peter,' said Colin. 'Can we have another soon – to tell you what happens at the police-station when Jack and I give them the third man's description?'

'Of course – tomorrow, same time,' said Peter. 'And I'll see if my mother will let us have tea down here in the shed. See you tomorrow then, Jack and Colin.'

They were just getting up when Scamper began to bark loudly and excitedly. Then there came a loud knock at the door, which made them all jump.

'Open in the name of the law,' said a strange, deep voice.

'Gracious – it's the police again,' said Colin, and opened the door.

There was no one there! The Seven stared out into the half-darkness, feeling just a bit scared. Scamper raced out, barking, and stopped by a bush. Peter ran up to it, and shone his torch there. A delighted giggle greeted him.

'*Susie!*' yelled everyone, in a fury.

'Please, Peter, I've brought poor Jack's bicycle for him to ride home on,' said the maddening Susie. 'I thought he'd be pleased.'

'You horrid little snooper!' shouted Jack. But Susie had gone, slipping away in the darkness. How much had she heard? *What* a little wretch she was!

CHAPTER NINE

Susie really is annoying

COLIN AND Jack cycled off to the police-station at once, Jack with his precious notebook in his pocket. When they got to the station, they found the sergeant there, a man they liked very much. He had already seen Colin twice – once when the police had gone to his granny's house, in answer to his telephone call, and once when they had called him out of school that morning, to ask him questions.

'Hallo, Colin – you again!' said the sergeant, and smiled. 'Well – got any more burglars to report?'

'No, sir,' said Colin. 'But Jack here has the description of the third man – the one Greta didn't see.'

'Well, I'm blessed!' said the sergeant, and pulled a note-pad in front of him. 'We've got pretty good descriptions of two of the men, but not the third. Greta didn't see him, as you just now said. How do *you* know what he was like? You said you didn't see anyone yourself, at the house.'

'No, sir,' said Colin. 'You see, it's like this. We were out in the woods last Saturday, and we came to a hut, and inside were three men. They were pretty awful to us and we thought they might be up to some mischief. So Jack here wrote down their descriptions. Jack, give your notes to the sergeant.'

Jack handed them over. The sergeant read them quickly. He whistled when he came to

197

'One was big and fat, and had a moustache. No hat. Gingery hair.' He put the notebook down and looked at Jack.

'Good work, son,' he said. 'Really, kids are pretty smart nowadays! Your description of two of them is excellent – we're pretty certain we know who they are, though we don't know *where* they are. I can't place the third one – the big, fat fellow, with a moustache and gingery hair. What was he dressed in? Did you notice?'

'Well no,' said Jack, trying to remember. 'They were all pretty dirty and scruffy. Nothing outstanding in their clothes, as far as I can remember. Did you notice anything in the way they were dressed, Colin?'

'No. I just think they were in overcoats of some sort,' said Colin, frowning. 'Two of them wore hats or, caps – and I know one hadn't a hat – that was the red-haired man, of course. We all noticed his hair, because he had no hat.'

'Well, this is a great help,' said the sergeant, giving Jack back his notebook. 'I expect those thieves are miles away by now, but keep your eyes open, will you – you and the others?'

'We certainly will, sir,' said both boys

together. They said goodnight, and left the police-station, both feeling very thrilled at having been able to help.

'We'll tell the others all this at the meeting tomorrow night,' said Jack. 'Gosh, I'll have to race home! I've loads of homework to do. Wait till I see that sister of mine – pretending she was the police tonight, and making us open our shed-door to her! Perhaps she won't interfere so much in future though – she's having two friends to stay with her   both girls, whose mother's in hospital. Susie will be so busy looking after them that she won't have time to interfere with the Secret Seven.'

'Good thing!' said Colin, who heartily disliked the aggravating Susie. 'We don't want her poking her nose into this!'

They parted and went their separate ways. Jack went to find Susie as soon as he got home, to tick her off for breaking in on their meeting that night.

'Susie!' he yelled, as soon as he got in. 'Where are you? What do you mean by pretending to . . . oh, sorry, I thought you were Susie!'

'No, I'm Doris, who's come to stay,' said the girl he had thought was Susie. 'And this is Hilda, my sister. It's nice of your mother to have us. I hope we shan't be in the way.'

Jack looked at Doris and Hilda, and he didn't much like what he saw. They grinned at him impudently, he thought, and he didn't look forward to having *three* giggling girls talking about him, and nudging each other, and playing jokes on him. One was bad enough!

'Open in the name of the law!' said a voice – Susie's, of course. 'Oh, Jack – did you really think I . . .'

'You behaved abominably,' said Jack. 'Breaking in on our meeting like that. I was ashamed of you.'

'We're going to make a little club ourselves – Hilda, Doris and I,' said Susie. 'It's called the Tiresome Three.'

'I should think it's a very good name,' said Jack. 'So long as you don't make yourselves tiresome to *us*, and keep away when we're meeting.'

'Oh, the grand Secret Seven!' said Susie.

She turned to the giggling Hilda and Doris. 'You've no idea how solemn their silly old meetings are,' she said. 'Passwords, badges, nobody else allowed in, oh, they think they're too grand for words. You look out, Jack – the Tiresome Three might come and join you one night!'

'Shall we raid their shed?' said Doris. 'That's what my brother and his club did to another club – they got a lot of things, they got . . .'

'If you *dare* to interfere with us, *any* of you, I'll – I'll pull your hair off!' cried Jack, exasperated, and marched out of the room, boiling over.

'What a bad-tempered brother you've got, Susie,' he heard Hilda say, and he very nearly turned back to pull her hair. He went to his room and sat down, frowning. Never mind! *Let* them laugh and giggle! The Secret Seven were helping the police, and he couldn't see the Tiresome Three helping *any*one!

'I'll have to warn the Seven that Susie and the others mean to make trouble,' he thought, as he took his homework from his school bag. 'Thank goodness we've got old

Scamper – he always barks when anyone comes near the shed. How *dare* Susie do the things she does!'

CHAPTER TEN

A wonderful guy

PETER ASKED his mother if he could have the
Secret Seven to tea the next day, Wednesday.

'You see, Mother, what with one thing and
another, there seems to be a lot to talk about
and plan – Bonfire Night, of course, and now

this business of Colin's granny being robbed, and us having seen the three men . . .'

'We'll see to the tea ourselves, Mother, you don't need to do a thing,' said Janet. 'And we won't scamp our homework, we promise you.'

'All right, dears – of course you can have a Secret Seven tea,' said their mother. 'I'll cut the bread and butter, and I'll bake you some biscuits, and you can buy some buns or something at the baker's. I shan't have time to make cakes too. Do you want lemonade or tea?'

'Oh, lemonade – no, orangeade for a change!' said Peter. *'We'll* carry everything down, Mother, and we'll wash up, too. You're always so *decent* about the Secret Seven.'

'Well, if you want to know something – I'm very glad I've got a decent son, who runs a decent club, helped by a very decent sister!' said Mother, laughing.

Everyone was very punctual at the meeting, and their eyes shone when they saw the spread provided for them.

'I'm glad I didn't eat too much dinner today,' said Colin, eyeing the currant bread and butter, and the jam sandwich that Janet had bought, and the big plate of home-made biscuits.

They talked as they munched away at their tea, Scamper gnawing happily at a great big bone. Jack told them about Susie and the Tiresome Three. Peter groaned.

'*Don't* say they're going to play silly tricks on us – really, I'm getting awfully tired of Susie,' he said.

'Well, it doesn't much matter if they raid us while we're *here*,' said Janet. 'The door's locked. And if they come when we're not here, the door will still be locked! Even Susie wouldn't break the window, surely, to get in!'

'How are you getting on with the guy?' asked Jack.

'We'll show you, when we begin the meeting,' said Janet. 'We've got some fine clothes for him! Pam's father was great. When he heard about the guy, he rummaged through his old clothes, and sent some.'

'You see, Dad's big and rather fat,' said Pam. 'So his clothes should fit the guy beautifully.'

'And George's father gave George a wonderful cap for the guy,' said Janet. 'Your father must have an awfully big head, George – the cap's enormous.'

'He *has* got a big head,' said George, proudly. 'It needs to be big, he's terribly brainy, you know.'

'And our dad gave us some old gum boots – his field boots, simply colossal,' said Peter. 'They might be too big even for the fat legs of the guy!'

'We'll dress him up after the meeting,' said Janet. 'He's there, waiting at the back – he'll be glad to be dressed. He needs a mask, too.'

'I'll slip up to the shops and get one as soon as I've finished tea,' said Colin. 'I don't like guys without faces – they look horrid. I bet old Scamper won't like the mask, though!'

'I hope you've all remembered to bring a little firework money,' said Peter.

'Yes,' said everyone, and Peter grinned, very pleased. He couldn't help thinking that his club must be about the best in the kingdom! Even their dog always behaved well!

The boys carried back the tea-things when tea was over. Then they settled down to the meeting, and Peter took the firework money from each member. He added up the total. 'Whew! Ten pounds fifty – pretty good, you know – and there's still some time to go. We mustn't forget we've still got to build our bonfire higher.'

'We can collect more wood on Saturday morning,' said George. 'Now, what about dressing the guy?'

They pulled the fat, shapeless body out from its rubber sheet, and sat it on a box. Scamper growled at it at once. He didn't like it at all.

They began to dress it, laughing. It wasn't at all easy.

'It seems as if the old guy just *won't* help us!' panted Jack, trying to pull a pair of enormous trousers over the guy's plump legs. 'Don't be so *awkward*, guy!'

'It's a good thing Pam's father is such a big man,' said Barbara. 'The guy is larger than we thought! What about some braces?'

'Oh, we don't need those. We can safety-pin the trousers to his body,' said Janet. 'There, the trousers are on at last – they make him more real, somehow.'

'Now the coat,' said Jack, taking up a rather stained old tweed coat, that didn't match the trousers.

'That's the coat my dad used when he was plastering and painting our kitchen,' said Pam. 'My mother said she was glad to see the back of it! Aren't the buttons nice? Half-yellow and half-brown. Too good for the guy, really!'

'Well, it fits him beautifully,' said Peter, laughing as he did up the buttons. 'Feeling warmer now, Mr Guy? Colin, what about you going to buy a mask before the shops shut?'

'Right,' said Colin, and slipped out of the shed door. 'Shan't be long.'

The others began to pull the boots on to the guy's plump legs. It really was a hard job.

'He's an obstinate fellow, this guy,' said Jack.

'Wants to go bare-foot, I suppose! There – that boot's on, thank goodness. Stop growling, Scamper. Anyone would think you didn't like our beautiful guy!'

Scamper's growls suddenly became louder and he ran to the door. 'Susie! The Tiresome Three!' said everyone. But they were wrong.

It was Colin, carrying a mask, and in a great state of excitement. He waved an evening paper at them.

'Hey! There's news about the thieves who got into my granny's house. They've caught two of them. It's all printed here. Stop messing about with the guy, and listen.'

'Shut the door,' said Peter, sharply, afraid that Susie might be lurking outside, and Colin banged it at once. He sat down on a box, and opened the paper. 'It's here – in the stop press news – this bit in the corner,' he said. 'I'll read it to you.'

CHAPTER ELEVEN

One up to the Tiresome Three

'Go on – do read it,' said Janet, impatiently.

'*It is reported this afternoon that two of the thieves who robbed Mrs Strangeway's house on Monday night, have been caught by the police. They had not left the district. The third man ran away and escaped. The police have a full description of him. He is stout, tall and has a moustache and red hair. Unfortunately the stolen articles have not yet been recovered. Anyone having seen a man of the above description is asked to contact the police.*'

'Gosh!' said Peter, as Colin finished reading. 'So they've got two of the men already. What a pity the other man escaped.'

'Yes – and took the stuff with him, I

suppose,' said Colin gloomily. 'My poor old granny is in an awful state, as you can imagine. She had to go to bed with shock as soon as she got back, and my mother sent for the doctor. If only she could get back the things she prized most – my grandfather's silver cups – the ones he won for all kinds of sport – and the jewellery that's been in her family for years. I wish the police had got the stolen stuff instead of the robbers!'

'Probably the two thieves who were caught will soon confess where they hid it,' said Pam.

'Well, I should think the third man, who wasn't caught, will certainly go and take the things from whatever hiding-place they are in now, and hide them somewhere else!' said Peter. 'Just in case his pals gave away the hiding-place! He could then wait a bit till all the hue and cry had died down, and take them for himself!'

'Yes, I suppose he could,' said Colin, laying down the paper. 'Fancy the men still being in the district. You'd have thought they would have got away as soon as possible.'

'I bet the man who's free will have put a hundred miles between himself and the police by now,' said Jack.

'If he hasn't, he'll find it difficult to move about in the daytime,' said Colin. 'You can shave off a moustache, but you can't hide your fatness – or your ginger hair.'

'You *can* hide your hair – dye it, say – or wear a hat, silly,' said Barbara.

'Let's get on with the guy,' said Janet. 'What do you think of him, Colin?'

She and Pam pulled the guy in front of Colin. He looked very strange in his big trousers, carefully safety-pinned in place, his enormous dirty old tweed coat, and large rubber boots. Scamper began to bark angrily, again.

'He simply can't bear our guy,' said Pam. 'Did you get a mask, Colin? Oh yes, there it is.

Put it on the guy, then we can put the cap on his head.'

Colin carefully fitted the big mask over the front of the guy's head. Everyone roared with laughter. The guy seemed very real now he had a face!

'Isn't it odd – you've chosen a mask with a red moustache!' said Janet. 'Like the robber who got away! Mr Guy Fawkes, are you sure you're not the third robber?'

The guy stared solemnly at her, and Scamper growled again. He really did not like the guy at all.

'Take the mask off and squeeze the head a bit to make the mask fit better,' said George. 'It sticks out over his chest too much.'

They took off the mask, and pummelled the stuffed head till it was a better shape. Then on went the mask again, and Scamper gave another volley of angry barks.

'Now the cap,' said George, and solemnly placed it on the guy's head, screwing it round a bit to give it a jaunty, rakish look. The Seven laughed uproariously. The guy looked really comical with his cap on.

'How do you do, Mr Fawkes?' said George, and shook him by the hand. 'I hope you are feeling well, and looking forward to warming yourself on our bonfire next week.'

'He looks awfully uncomfortable sitting on that box,' said Janet. 'And he's heavy to hold up straight. Can't we get him an old chair, or something, to sit in? He'll last a lot longer on top of the bonfire if he's sitting up.'

'I think there's an old chair, with arms, in the stables,' said Peter. 'Nobody uses it now. Let's go and get it, shall we?'

They all trooped out of the shed, Scamper too, leaving the guy sprawled over his box.

'Back in a minute, Mr Fawkes,' said Colin, politely, and made the others laugh.

They made their way to the stables, and there sure enough, in a corner with other jumble, was the old chair. Its cane seat was almost gone, and part of the back. But it still had its two arms.

'Just the thing,' said Peter, pleased. 'We can easily put a bit of wood over the rotten cane seat, for him to sit on. Give me a hand, Colin.'

They took the old chair back to the shed,

Peter shining his torch as they went. When they came in sight of the shed, glowing by the light of its little oil-lamp, they stopped in a hurry!

Peter's torch had picked up something standing against the shed, near the open door. Whatever – whoever – was it?'

'It's – it's our *guy*!' cried Janet in fright. 'Look – he's walked out of the shed – he's standing there! Peter! Look at him!'

Yes, there was the guy, sure enough, leaning against the shed, quite still, his mask looking exactly like a face. And then –

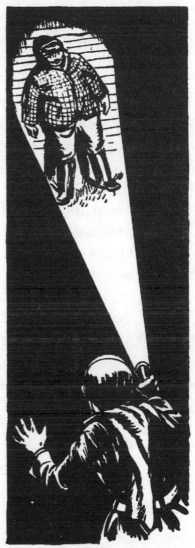

and then came the sound of suppressed giggles from somewhere nearby!

'*Susie!*' yelled Jack, in fury. 'You've taken our guy and stood him outside. Wait till I get you three – how *dare* you!'

There came the sound of more giggles, and then scampering feet. The Tiresome Three, having made their first raid, were gone!

'They've hung him on a nail, look,' said Peter, angrily seeing that the guy's neck was neatly impaled on an old nail at just about the right height. 'Gosh – didn't he look real, leaning there against the shed? What on earth possessed us to go off and leave the door open? We must have been mad!'

'Wait till I get home,' said Jack, grimly. 'I'll tick those girls off properly. Here – let's take the guy into the shed again. Come along, Mr Fawkes. Sorry you've had such a silly trick played on you, poor old man!'

CHAPTER TWELVE

Jack can be tiresome too!

THE SECRET Seven were really very angry to think that the Tiresome Three had actually dared to go into their meeting-shed, and take out the guy.

'What idiots we were to leave the shed open, even for those few minutes!' groaned Peter. 'But Scamper didn't bark or growl as he usually does when there's anyone hiding near.'

'I expect they arrived at the very minute we went off to get the chair,' said Colin. 'Just a bit of sheer luck for them, that's all. For goodness' sake lock the door each time you leave the shed, Peter. They'll steal the whole guy next, and burn him on their own bonfire. Are they going to have a bonfire, Jack?'

'Don't ask *me*,' said Jack. 'As if they'd tell me anything! Those two girls, Doris and Hilda, are even worse than Susie, it seems to me! Giggle, giggle, giggle, all the time. I expect they *will* have fireworks and a bonfire – I don't know about a guy.'

They sat the guy down in the chair, having first put a sheet of wood under him to stop him sinking down through the broken cane seat. He sat there, his arms on the arms of the chair, looking as if he wanted to smoke a pipe or read a newspaper!

'He's not a bad guy at all,' said Barbara. 'I've never seen such a nice *plump* one before. We could perhaps get him an old pipe – we could stick it into his mouth for him.'

'Gosh – it's getting pretty late,' said George, looking at his watch. 'I've got homework to do. I must go. That was a very good meeting, even if it had an annoying ending. Don't forget to thank your mother for us, Peter. Jolly fine tea!'

The meeting broke up, for not only George had homework to do. Soon the shed was in darkness, the door securely locked and the key in Peter's pocket. The guy sat there in his chair alone.

Jack cycled back home, fuming with rage. Susie really was behaving badly. What a sister to have! He went to put his bicycle away, and suddenly spotted a faint light in the summer-house down the garden.

'Hallo – who's there?' he thought, and crept down to see. He heard low voices, and recognised them at once.

'Susie – and the others! A meeting of the Tiresome Three, I suppose!' thought Jack, grimly. 'All right – *I'll* do a little snooping this time!'

He stood close to the windows of the summer-house, thinking that it was a remarkably cold spot to choose for a meeting-place. He grinned to himself. What a fine revenge for Susie's surprise that night!

He heard Susie's voice. 'We can't let the Seven crow over us with a guy like that and the biggest bonfire in the district!' she said. 'I wouldn't mind if they'd let us *share* in the fireworks and *see* the bonfire, and help to burn the guy – but they're so mean, all of

them, and they just won't share a thing.'

'Well, we'll raid them again,' said a voice –
it sounded like Hilda's. 'What about their
bonfire? Where is it? Can't we raid that?'

'I don't know where it is,' said Susie. 'I can
find out, though. I'll ask Jack quite nicely – and
I bet he'll tell me!'

There were a few giggles, and something that
Jack couldn't catch. He began to boil with fury.
Raid the Secret Seven's *bonfire*! What a nerve!

'It's a pity we've so little money for fireworks,'
said Doris. 'They're so dreadfully expensive –

and it's no fun unless you have a lot. And we haven't a guy, either.'

'It's not much good having a guy unless you've got a bonfire to burn him on,' said Susie. 'Didn't their guy have marvellous clothes? I wish we could get hold of some like that!'

Then came more talk that Jack couldn't hear. The Tiresome Three must have put their heads close together, and were making plans. *What* plans? Jack had great forebodings. What were these awful girls going to do next? He *certainly* wouldn't tell them where the bonfire was! Well, he might *hint* – but it would be a hint that would send them quite in the wrong direction!

Jack began to smile. Yes – he could send the Tiresome Three on a long, long walk – with no bonfire at the end of it! It would serve them right.

Then he thought he would give the girls a fright to pay them back for their night's mischief. He opened his mouth and gave a weird and wonderful groan that startled even himself.

'Oooo-ah-oooo-ee-AHHHH!'

There was a sudden silence in the summer-house. Then he heard Susie's scared voice. 'Goodness! Whatever was that?'

Jack groaned again, ending with a most bloodcurdling yowl. With three terrified shrieks the Tiresome Three stumbled out of the summerhouse and fled up the garden at top speed. Jack went into the summer-house and collapsed on the seat, holding his sides with laughter.

'Oh my! I really didn't know I could groan like that!' he said. 'Well – I'll saunter into the house now, and pretend I've just come from the Secret Seven meeting.'

So in he strolled, hands in his pockets, humming a tune. The girls turned to him at once, still looking scared.

'Jack! Did you hear a perfectly awful noise as you came in through the garden?' asked Susie.

'What do you mean? The cat mewing?' said Jack. 'Don't say you're scared of *him*! Or do you mean the old brown owl? You girls! If you heard a mouse squeak you'd skitter off in fright! And by the way, I suppose you think that was funny, taking our guy out of the shed like that? Well, it wasn't. It was just plain mean.'

'Well, aren't *you* mean?' demanded Susie at once. 'You won't share your guy and we haven't one. You won't share your fireworks – and we've none! And I bet you won't even tell us where your bonfire will be – you won't even let us *see* that!'

'Where *is* the bonfire?' said Hilda, looking very innocent. 'Fancy not even telling us that!'

'Oh, I'll tell you where you'll find a bonfire we've built,' said Jack 'You know Haylings Field, that runs up that very steep hill? Well, you'll find a bonfire there, all ready to light. Now don't you be mean and light it! I don't trust you three giggling idiots an inch!'

He strolled out of the room, and the Tiresome Three grinned at one another.

'Easy, wasn't it?' said Susie. 'We'll get there tomorrow! *And* we'll pull their bonfire to bits!'

CHAPTER THIRTEEN

Face at the window

JACK CYCLED round to Peter's early the next morning to tell him the joke he meant to play on the Tiresome Three. Peter grinned.

'Jolly good idea! I'll cycle up Haylings Hill with you now, and we'll take a few miserable twigs – and a note to put under them! When will the girls go up, do you think?'

'After afternoon school, I imagine,' said Jack. 'Only Susie has a bike, so they'll have to climb all the way up on foot – and you know how steep it is.'

'I'll write a note now,' said Peter, getting out his notebook and pencil. He scribbled something and signed it, then passed it across to Jack.

'YOU CAN HAVE THE WHOLE OF THIS
BONFIRE IF YOU LIKE. HOPE YOU
ENJOYED YOUR CLIMB. A GOOD
LAUGH FROM – THE SECRET SEVEN.'

Jack chuckled. 'Wonderful. That will make
them wild – they'll have all that long climb for
nothing! All the same, we'll have to keep an
eye on our *real* bonfire, Peter. I wouldn't be in
the least surprised if they didn't come and look
for it and kick it about, when they find they've
been tricked into going up to the top of Haylings
Hill.'

'Yes. We'll certainly keep an eye on it. One
or other of us had better keep guard there, I

suppose,' said Peter. 'What's today – Thursday. We'll all meet this afternoon, I think, and we'll take what money anyone brings. Dad says we can go with him to get the fireworks this week. Better not leave it too late or the best ones will be gone. Let's see, Bonfire Night is on Sunday – that means we'll have to hold it on Monday.'

'Why not Saturday?' asked Jack.'

'Colin said he might not be able to come,' said Peter. 'He asked me *not* to make it Saturday. I'd better get my bike and ride up Haylings Hill with you straight away, or we'll be late for school. Gather a few sticks and twigs while I get it.'

Soon the two boys were cycling off at top speed. In their bicycle baskets was a collection of small twigs. They grinned when they looked at them.

Haylings Hill was very steep indeed. They had to get off their bicycles near the top and push them. At last they were at the summit, and hurriedly arranged a criss-cross of twigs as if for a small fire. Peter stuffed the note under the twigs, so that a corner of it showed.

'There! I hope the Tiresome Three will enjoy

their climb!' he said. 'Come on – it's getting late. Thank goodness it's all downhill now!'

The Secret Seven met again in their shed that day at a quarter past five, when everyone had had tea. Scamper was delighted to see them, and leapt round in delight. He couldn't imagine why the Seven were meeting again so soon, but he was certainly glad to welcome them. The little oil lamp was lit, and the shed looked warm and cosy.

The guy sat sedately in his chair while Peter collected a little more money. 'Fifteen pounds,' he announced. 'Great. Now, who'd like to come and choose the fireworks? Dad is going to the shops at dinner time tomorrow. He said that three of us could go – and the rest can say now if there are any particular fireworks they'd like us to get.'

It was decided that George and Pam should go with Peter. Then Jack, grinning all over his face, told the Seven how he had done a bit of snooping on the Tiresome Three, and heard their threats of raiding the bonfire – and how he had told them they would find a bonfire laid on the top of Haylings Hill.

'And we went up there this morning, Peter and I, and put a silly little twig fire ready, with a note from the Secret Seven!' he said. 'I bet the Tiresome Three have taken a long walk up there after afternoon school today!'

'They'll be furious,' said Janet. 'I hope they won't come and raid *our* bonfire.'

'I don't think they know where it is at present,' said Jack. 'As soon as I hear that they do know – or are looking for it – I'll tell you. Then we can be on our guard.'

'Grrrrrr!' said Scamper, suddenly, and made them all jump.

'Can it be the Tiresome Three back from the hill *already*?' said Jack, startled. 'What's up, Scamper?'

'Grrrrrr!' said Scamper again, and all the hairs on his neck rose up. He ran to the door and listened intently.

Pam suddenly gave a loud shriek, and made everyone jump violently. Janet turned on her angrily. 'What did you scream like that for? That's just what the Tiresome Three want – to scare us and make us yell out!'

Pam pointed to the little shed window with a

shaking finger. 'A face looked in there,' she said. 'I saw it.'

'Then it *is* Susie and her friends!' said Jack, fiercely. 'Why didn't we draw the curtain across?'

They all ran to the door and pulled it open, and Scamper ran out, barking. He sniffed all round, and then stood still, growling again.

'They've gone,' said Peter, shining his torch all round. 'Perhaps they came to raid the guy – take him away or something in revenge. Shut up, Scamper. There's nobody here now.'

They all went back and Peter drew the curtain across the window. 'Better break up the meeting now,' he said. 'Meet here on Saturday morning, please, and we'll finish building the bonfire. Jack, tell Susie we saw her – or one of the others – peering in. And tell her we hope they enjoyed their long walk!'

'I will,' said Jack, and cycled off. To his great astonishment he met Susie, Hilda and Doris at his front gate, walking wearily into the drive. Doris was almost in tears.

'You beast!' said Susie, angrily. 'Sending us all the way up there, to the top of Haylings Hill! That silly little bonfire – and the horrid note. Doris has hurt her ankle, falling on the hill – she could hardly get home. You're *mean*!'

'But – but wasn't it you, then, peering in at our shed window?' said Jack amazed.

'I don't know what you're talking about,' said Susie. 'So don't try and be funny. I tell you, we've only just got back – and I'll have to see to poor Doris's ankle *at once*.'

They went round to the garden door, leaving Jack feeling puzzled – and rather sorry for his trick. He really hadn't meant anyone to fall down the hill.

But *who* had looked through the window? He had better telephone Peter immediately!

CHAPTER FOURTEEN

A dreadful shock

JACK TELEPHONED Peter as soon as he had a chance. 'Peter? I say – it *wasn't* Susie or her friends who came and peeped in at our window tonight. They'd only just got back from Haylings Hill when I arrived home. Doris had hurt her ankle and was limping.'

Peter whistled. 'Who was it, then? Wait a minute, here's Dad. Dad – I say, Dad – you didn't peep in at our shed window tonight, did you?'

'No,' said his father. 'But the gardener was working late today – I expect he saw your light there, and peeped in.'

'Oh – so that was it,' said Peter, and told Jack. 'Anyway, the shed's locked,' he said. 'No one can get in. See you tomorrow, Jack.'

Susie was very, very angry about Jack's trick. 'I've a good mind to tell Mother,' she scolded. 'You should just *see* poor Doris's ankle. Well, you just look out for yourselves, you mean, horrible Seven. We're going to find your bonfire and pull it to bits! And if only we can get hold of your guy, we'll take him and burn him ourselves!'

'Don't be silly,' said Jack. 'The shed's locked, you know that. Yes, I know you found it unlocked the other night, but that was only for a few minutes while we went to get a chair for the guy. I tell you, I'm sorry about Doris's ankle. Now leave me in peace.'

But Susie wouldn't, and poor Jack had to retire to his bedroom. He wished once again that he and Peter hadn't played that trick on Susie and the others. Once Susie made up her mind to pay him back for anything, she usually did! Suppose she found their big bonfire? That would be the end of it!

Next day Peter, George and Pam went off with Peter's father to buy the fireworks. They managed to get all they wanted, except for some called Moon Rockets.

232

'They'll be in tomorrow morning,' said the shop-woman. 'You call for them then. And I'll have some in called "Catch-me-if-you-can" – little ones that rush about in the air, and hop all over the ground.'

'Oh, will you keep some for us, please?' asked Peter. 'We've saved fifteen pounds altogether – and we've spent just over ten pounds already. I'll take the rest of the money home and give it to Mum when she goes shopping tomorrow. She'll bring it in to you and take the fireworks back home. I'd certainly like some Moon Rockets!'

He put down ten pounds and fifty pence in silver, and Dad picked up the parcel of fireworks. He was going to lock them up in a safe place when he got home. George and Pam had helped to choose them and were very pleased. Peter put the rest of the money into his pocket.

'Four pounds fifty,' he said. 'I'll make a note of what we've spent when I get back home, and put the change into the box on the shelf. If anyone has any more firework money they can add to it when we meet to make the bonfire bigger tomorrow morning. There's no meeting tonight.'

He popped into the shed when he got back, and put the money away safely. He took a look at the guy, and decided to ask his father for an old pipe. 'We didn't do anything about that,' he thought. 'And he *does* look as if a pipe would suit him!'

He asked his father later on in the evening. 'A pipe? Well, my old pipes are my favourite ones really,' said his father. 'Still, wait a minute. I've got one with a broken stem. Your guy won't mind that, I'm sure.'

He found it and gave it to Peter. Scamper ran to the door and barked.

'Take him for a turn round the garden with you,' said Peter's mother.

'Right!' said Peter. 'Come on, Scamper – walkies! We'll take the pipe to the guy. Coming, Janet?'

'Got the key of the shed?' asked Janet. Peter fumbled in his pocket. Then he felt in his other pocket.

'Bother!' he said. 'Where is it? Gosh – surely I locked up the shed when I popped in with the money. Oh, *don't* say I left the key in the lock!'

'Quick – come and see,' said Janet, thinking at once of the Tiresome Three. They pulled on coats and tore down the garden to the shed, Scamper leaping about madly. They came to the door, and Peter shone his torch on the lock.

'Look – I *did* leave the key in it,' he said. 'What an absolute idiot I am! I really don't *deserve* to be the leader of the Secret Seven. Thank goodness Susie hasn't been along and taken it!'

He unlocked the door and they went into the shed, Peter holding the pipe for the guy. Janet gave a sudden yell and clutched his arm.

'Peter! *Peter!* Look at the guy! His clothes are gone! Susie *has* been here. Oh, why ever did you leave the key in the lock?'

Sure enough, the guy sat in his chair, wearing his mask and nothing else. He looked very foolish and fat as he sprawled there.

'The only thing the Tiresome Three have left him are the safety pins that pinned his trousers,' said Janet, tearfully. 'Oh, Peter! Our lovely guy – the best one we've ever had! Whatever will the others say?'

Peter was simply horrified. To think that this was all his fault! He looked round the shed, hoping vainly to find the clothes thrown into a corner. But no – there wasn't even the cap to be seen.

'Come back to the house,' he said, dolefully, and locked the door carefully, putting the key into his pocket. 'This is simply awful. I'll get on to Jack straight away and tell him what the Tiresome Three have done.'

Jack was just as horrified as Peter and Janet when he heard the news. He could hardly believe his ears.

'So *that's* where Susie and the others went this evening, is it?' he said. 'I thought they were having one of their silly meetings down in the summer-house, but they must have gone to our shed. Well – I'll go for Susie over this!'

He slammed down the receiver and went to find Susie. She and Hilda and Doris were sitting by the fire, reading. Jack exploded angrily.

'What have you done with our guy's clothes? So *that's* where you disappeared to this evening – you went stealing!'

'Don't be funny,' said Susie, looking most astonished. 'We were up in the attic all evening, looking out jumble for Mother's sale.'

'You were *not*!' shouted Jack. 'Don't tell untruths. WHERE ARE THOSE CLOTHES?'

CHAPTER FIFTEEN

Oh, that Tiresome Three!

SUSIE AND Doris and Hilda looked quite alarmed when Jack shouted so loudly.

'I tell you,' began Susie, raising her voice too, 'I tell you *we* haven't got the clothes – but I'm really glad to hear your silly old guy has lost them. Ha ha!'

'Where did you hide the clothes?' shouted

Jack again – and at that moment his mother put her head into the room.

'Jack! Stop shouting. What's the matter?'

'Susie and Doris and Hilda have taken the clothes off our guy,' blurted out Jack, forgetting that it was a mean trick to tell tales. But he did feel so very, very angry! 'And they are telling fibs about it. Oh yes you are, Susie, I know you!'

'That's enough,' said his mother. 'Go up to your room, Jack, and cool off. I'll speak to Susie.'

Jack stamped out of the room, boiling with rage. He looked into Susie's room, hoping to see the guy's clothes stuffed under the bed or in the wardrobe, but there was nothing there. He went into his own room and waited.

Soon his mother came in.

'You are not to say another word to Susie and her friends about that guy's clothes,' she said. 'You've upset the girls very much – and Susie told me how you and Peter tricked them into climbing all the way up Haylings Hill. I'm ashamed of you.'

'But, *Mother*,' said Jack, 'please listen.

Mother, *please* ask Susie where she hid the guy's clothes.'

'I'm not going to discuss the subject at all,' said his mother, and shut the door. Jack sat and fumed. He didn't even dare to go down and telephone to Peter. He felt sure that the Tiresome Three would be giggling over his shoulder if he did.

The Seven had to meet at the shed the next morning – and it was a sad and sorry company! They gazed at their wonderful guy, now so bare and ugly, wearing only his mask, and Pam burst into tears.

'All the clothes I brought!' she sobbed. 'It's too bad! I think your mother ought to go to Susie's mother, Peter, and complain. It's *stealing*.'

'Well – not exactly,' said Jack, uncomfortably. 'I mean – I'm sure Susie will give them back after Bonfire Night, it's just one of her silly *tricks*. I was so angry last night I could have shaken her to bits.'

'It's all my fault, I'm afraid,' said Peter, humbly. 'If I hadn't left the key in the lock, it would never have happened. I take the whole blame. Susie just took her chance – it was a real bit of luck for her – just like when we left the door open to get the guy that chair. That was a bit of luck for her too.'

'Well – we'll have to try and get some more clothes,' said Colin. 'There's an old raincoat hanging in our garage. I'm sure nobody wants it. I'll get that. And somebody can surely get hold of another cap. The guy will just have to make do with those!'

'We chose the fireworks,' said Pam, changing the subject, very sorry for poor unhappy Peter. 'Fine ones! Peter's father has put them away safely. And we've kept some money back to get some of those new Moon Rockets when they come into the shop. How much money have we got left, Peter?'

'Four pounds fifty, I think,' said Peter, taking the money-box from the shelf. 'The money's here.' He shook the box, suddenly looking alarmed. He put it down quickly on the little table and took off the lid. Then he looked up, dismayed.

'The money's gone,' he said. 'Not a penny of it left. Four pounds fifty all gone!'

There was a dead silence. Even Scamper did not move an ear. Then Jack spoke, his words falling over one another.

'If Susie took it, it was only a joke, Peter. Really, it was. She – she's not a thief.'

'Well, didn't she steal the guy's clothes?' demanded Barbara. 'I wouldn't put anything past the Tiresome Three!'

'No, no, wait,' said Peter. 'I feel like Jack – I don't believe Susie would ever *steal*. After all, she's Jack's sister. I think she and the others may have taken the clothes and the money to pay us back – meaning to keep them till after Bonfire Night and then give them back . . .'

'Yes-yes, that's what they'll do,' said Janet. 'I'm sure of it. Jack, just tell Susie you know they've got our money, but you jolly well want it back after Bonfire Night. We shouldn't have had such a feud on between us. It's getting too silly for words.'

'All right,' said Jack. 'And now for goodness' sake let's go and collect wood for the bonfire. I can't sit here a moment longer. I feel too angry for words.'

They all got up and went out, Peter locking

the door very carefully indeed. They walked rather silently to the field and looked at their bonfire.

'Someone's been digging round and about it,' said George. 'I wonder what for.' He stamped down the rough clods, and looked at the bonfire. 'It wants a good bit more on!' he said. 'Cheer up, Jack, cheer up, Peter. You look as if you've done a whole page of sums wrong!'

Even that joke didn't bring a smile to anyone's face. What a blow to lose their guy's clothes *and* the rest of the firework money! What a blow that Peter hadn't locked the door last night!

They followed the same plan as before, collecting wood and piling it at the edge of the wood, then roping it and dragging it to the bonfire. It soon grew very big, and the Seven began to feel more cheerful when they thought what a blaze it would make. Scamper ran round with twigs in his mouth, looking very busy indeed. He even began to take them off the bonfire too, but that was soon stopped!

'Look – look, there's Susie and the others!' said George, suddenly. 'They must have been hunting about for our bonfire.'

'*Where are our guy's clothes?*' yelled Pam, suddenly remembering how much trouble she had gone to in getting them.

'We haven't got them!' shouted back Susie.

'You have!' cried Pam. 'Don't you go near our bonfire. We know you'd take that away too, if you could.'

244

'Be quiet, Pam,' said Janet.

'We don't want a silly bonfire like this,' shouted Susie. 'Why, it'll fall to pieces if it's kicked. Look!'

And to the Seven's horror she and Hilda and Doris ran round it, kicking away some of the twigs. *Well!* Whatever next!

CHAPTER SIXTEEN

Keep guard on the bonfire!

As soon as the Seven ran across the field towards the bonfire, Susie and the others disappeared.

'You wait!' called Susie. 'We'll come back, and you won't find much of your bonfire left!'

'We'll just have to put someone on guard,' said Peter, dolefully. 'I'm beginning to think it was a great mistake to quarrel with Susie. She's too clever.'

They finished the bonfire, keeping a good look-out for the Tiresome Three, but not another sign of them did they see.

'Better take it in turns to watch the bonfire this afternoon,' said George.

'No. I know a better idea than that,' said Jack.

'*I'll* watch Susie and the other girls. I won't let them out of my sight. And tonight I'll take them to the cinema, so that I know they'll not be up to mischief. Mother said she would give me the money for it. Mind you, I shan't *like* doing it, but it's the only sensible thing I can think of.'

'It's a very, very good idea,' said Janet. 'And it does mean we won't have to stand about in this cold field all day, watching the bonfire! Do you want Peter to keep you company tonight at the cinema? It would be rather awful for you to have those three girls all to yourself.'

'All right,' said Jack, gratefully. 'It would make things a bit easier.'

So that night Peter and Jack solemnly took the three giggling girls to the cinema. His mother was very pleased.

'I'm glad you've made up that silly quarrel,' she said to Jack. 'I knew the girls hadn't taken those clothes – it wouldn't be a bit like them to do a thing like that.'

Jack said nothing, but thought privately that it would be *exactly* like them. He had kept an eye on the three girls all the afternoon, and knew that they had not gone near the bonfire. And they would be safe under his wing at the cinema and until bedtime. That was something!

Next morning, which was Sunday, the three girls went to church, Jack with them. But in the afternoon Susie grew restive.

'Let's go for a walk,' she said to Hilda and Doris. Jack pricked up his ears at once. Ah – where to? The bonfire field?

'I'll go with you,' he said.

'No thanks,' said Susie. 'I don't particularly want to be under your eye any more. What do you think we are going to do? Kick your bonfire to pieces? I bet that's what you're thinking.'

As that was exactly what Jack *was* thinking, he couldn't help going red. And then, just at that moment, his father called him.

'Jack, old son, come and give me a hand with cleaning the car, will you?' he said.

'Er – well – I thought of going for a walk with the girls,' said poor Jack.

'*We* can spare him, Dad,' said Susie, with a wicked grin. 'So long, Jack. Be good!'

And away went the three girls, leaving Jack

to go out to the garage and begin hosing the car. Bother! Now he couldn't possibly keep an eye on them. Wait – hadn't he better telephone Peter and tell him to guard the bonfire? It would be so awful to have such a beauty spoilt now!

'Can I go and telephone Peter, Dad?' he asked his father. 'I've – er – just remembered something important.'

'Well, wait till you've finished the hosing,' said his father. 'It can't be so terribly important that you have to go at once!'

So, for three-quarters of an hour Jack worked on the car, fuming. Suppose Susie and the others were ruining the bonfire now? How maddening it would be! He was very glad to rush off to the telephone as soon as his father gave him permission.

'Peter? Is that you? Listen, Susie and the others have gone out for a walk – but it's just *possible* they may go to the bonfire field. Keep an eye there this afternoon, will you?'

'Right,' said Peter. 'Thanks for phoning.' He called to Janet. 'Hey, Janet – that was Jack. He says Susie and her friends have gone out for a walk – will we keep an eye on the bonfire.'

'Oh my goodness – we'd better go out into the field straight away!' said Janet, and flew to get her coat. Peter fetched his and they went into the garden, and down to the bottom. In a few minutes they were out in the bonfire field.

No one was there. The field was empty. Probably Susie had taken her friends quite a different way! Peter glanced at the bonfire.

What a shock he got! He clutched Janet's arm and pointed to the bonfire, unable to say a word. There was very little of the huge pile to be seen. It had been scattered over a wide area. Big twigs, little twigs, branches – there they lay on the grass.

'They've destroyed it,' said Janet, and tears came to her eyes. 'Oh, how *could* they? It was such a beauty too – so high and wide. Oh, Peter – why didn't Jack telephone sooner? We could so easily have driven Susie away.'

Peter was very red in the face. He stared at the ruined bonfire, his mouth set and angry. 'Susie must have gone mad,' he said at last, and marched over to what was left of the great heap.

'What's this hole?' said Janet, in surprise, as

they came up to where the bonfire had been built. 'It looks as if Susie and the others had a spade and scattered the wood everywhere and then dug a hole. Honestly, they must be mad! What are they up to, Peter?'

'I don't know,' said Peter, staring. 'Let's go and phone Jack. Wait a minute, though – surely that's Susie and her friends coming up the field! It *is*! Let's go and tackle them – let's see what they've got to say! Come on!'

CHAPTER SEVENTEEN

A spade – and a button!

PETER AND Janet met the Tiresome Three as they drew near the bonfire. Susie gazed at the ruined pile of wood in amazement.

'What's happened!' she said. 'Have you been kicking your bonfire about?'

'No – *you're* the ones who have done that,' said Peter, his voice trembling with anger.

'We've only just come!' said Doris, indignantly. 'You saw us!'

'So you say – but it's quite clear you've been here before,' said Peter. 'You're good at mean tricks, aren't you?'

Susie looked at him and then at the bonfire. 'Well, I won't say that we wouldn't have spoilt it a *bit*,' she said. 'But we wouldn't have

252

destroyed it like this – and who dug that hole in the middle?'

'Don't pretend,' said Peter, in disgust. Janet suddenly tugged at his arm.

'Peter – Peter, they're *not* pretending! They're just as surprised as we are! Peter, it *wasn't* them!'

'Peter won't believe you,' said Susie, scornfully. 'Jack won't, either. Well, it just happens to be the truth, see – we've *only – just – come!* So what about looking round and finding out who really *did* do all this?'

Peter and Janet stared at her. She spoke very earnestly indeed.

'You think we took your guy clothes, and your money – and now you think we've ruined

your bonfire. Well, we didn't. And that's the *truth*!'

And with that, Susie, Hilda and Doris marched off, heads in air, leaving Peter and Janet still staring, unable to say a word.

Janet found her tongue at last. She turned to Peter. 'Peter, they truly are not pretending. They certainly didn't ruin our bonfire – and I don't believe they did the other things either. Anyway, I never *could* believe that Susie took our money. It's someone else, Peter, *someone else* who is playing tricks!'

'But who?' said Peter, bewildered. 'And why steal the clothes off the guy? It seems such a mad thing to do.'

'Let's look round a bit,' said Janet. 'We might find footprints or something. And I wish I knew who had been digging about like this. It seems so *mad* somehow. Look at this big clod of earth thrown up. Do you suppose Mr Burton knows anything about it? He knew we were making a bonfire, because we asked him for the hedge trimmings to burn.'

'Well, yes – Mr Burton *might* have seen someone about!' said Peter. 'I wonder if he's around anywhere? He usually helps to milk the cows on Sunday, so that the cowman can get a bit of time off.'

'I think that's him over there,' said Janet looking in the direction of the wood. 'Perhaps he's going to his little hut. Let's go after him and ask him if he's seen anyone messing about in this field.'

They ran after the figure in the distance, but the man disappeared between the trees.

'Yes – I think it *is* Mr Burton,' said Peter. 'Come on – I bet he's gone to his hut!'

They made their way into the wood till they came to a little overgrown hut. They called loudly. 'Mr Burton! Mr Burton! Are you there?'

There was no answer.

'I'm going inside,' said Peter, and disappeared through the half-open doorway. Janet followed him.

'No – he's not here,' said Peter, looking round. It was rather dark in the shed, but his eyes grew used to the dimness, something caught his eye – something that glinted a little. He picked it up.

'A spade!' he said. 'And look, Janet – it's Mr Burton's! It's got his name burnt across the handle. He always burns his name on his tools, in case they get stolen.'

Janet looked distressed. 'Peter! You don't think it could be Mr *Burton* doing all these things, do you?' she said, anxiously. 'I like Mr Burton. But – but – *someone's* been messing about round our bonfire with a spade – and this one's got Mr Burton's name on it!'

'You mean it might have been Mr Burton peering in at our window, and walking in when the door was unlocked and taking the guy clothes for himself?' said Peter. 'He certainly needs a few decent clothes! And taking our money too! But we've had Mr Burton for *ages*, and Daddy thinks he's a wonder. It *can't* be old Mr Burton – unless he's gone mad!'

'Well, this is certainly his spade,' said Janet. 'Oh, I can't *bear* it to be Mr Burton! If we tell Daddy he'll lose his job.'

Peter looked round the hut again, puzzled and worried. It was bad enough to have thought that the Tiresome Three might have played mean tricks – but it was worse still to think of old Mr Burton doing such peculiar things!

He saw something small and round lying on the floor, and picked it up.

'A button,' he said. 'Look, Janet – it seems familiar, somehow. Do you recognise it?'

Yes, Janet did! 'Of *course*, don't you remember? The guy's old tweed coat had buttons like this – half-yellow and half-brown! The thief has been here – sat down here – and a button fell off the coat. I expect he was wearing it. Peter, who in the world is it? That coat's too big for Mr Burton, surely.'

'He *could* have had it altered,' said Peter. 'Come on – let's go home. There's something odd about all this.'

CHAPTER EIGHTEEN

Jack has a sudden idea

PETER AND Janet went home feeling rather upset and extremely puzzled.

'Better tell all the others tomorrow at school what has happened,' said Peter. 'If they could each bring something to eat, and Mother would let us have lemonade again, we could have a quick tea, and then go out and rebuild the bonfire. We've got the guy all right, and Dad got the fireworks – not as many as we hoped, but still, enough to have a bit of fun.'

'Yes, it's disappointing that our grand plan for a wonderful guy and a huge bonfire has been spoilt – but we'll just have to make do with second best,' said Janet.

So, after afternoon school on Monday, the

Seven met once again in the shed, with Scamper to welcome them as usual. The girls had been told by Janet at school what had happened the day before, and the boys had been told by Peter. They sat down, opened their bags of cakes and biscuits, and accepted lemonade from Peter.

'Well,' began Peter, 'you know more or less what happened to our bonfire yesterday – *ab*solutely ruined – and you know that Janet and I think it wasn't Susie and her friends after all.'

'You said it was probably Mr Burton, the old hedger-and-ditcher,' said Colin.

'Well, it wasn't,' said Peter, and this was news to everyone but Janet. 'My father happened to mention him this morning, and said he had been ill for some days and in bed. So it certainly *wasn't* him.'

'Probably some tramp then, who peered into our shed, saw the nice warm clothes the guy was wearing, and stole them – and the money too,' said Jack. 'But what *I* can't understand is, who ruined our bonfire – and what's the sense of making holes round it?'

There was a silence – and then, quite suddenly Jack smacked his hand down so hard on his knee that everyone jumped almost out of their skins.

'We're blind!' said Jack. 'We're idiots! We're complete fools!'

The others stared at him in alarm. Whatever did he mean!

'Hold on, Jack, old thing,' said Peter. 'What's up? You look as if you've seen a ghost or something!'

'Well, I haven't. But I think I've spotted the person who's been stealing our things and spoiling our plans!' said Jack. 'Of course, of course, of *course*!'

'Who is it?' demanded Peter.

'Well, who could it be but the third thief who escaped when the other two were caught – the ones who robbed Colin's granny!' said Jack. 'Don't you *see*?'

'The third thief – but . . .' began Peter.

'Yes! He knew the police had a full description of him, it said so in the papers! So he had to get other clothes – *and he got them from our guy*!' said Jack.

'Of course! Don't you remember, he was tall
and fat!' said Janet. 'He'd need big clothes –
and he must have spotted them on our guy . . .'

'Yes – that time he peeped in at our window!'
half shouted George. 'It wasn't the gardener or
Mr Burton, it must have been that thief!'

'He needed money – and took ours!' said
Barbara.

'And do you know what I think? I bet the
other two thieves buried the stolen valuables in
our field!' cried Peter. 'And that's what all the

261

digging's for – those holes – those thrown-up clods! He stole Mr Burton's spade for that!'

'And since Mr Burton's been ill, the thief must have been sleeping in his old hut!' put in Pam. 'And that's how that button came there – he was wearing the guy's coat and it came off.'

Scamper felt the excitement round him and began to bark, wagging his tail hard. Peter patted him.

'Quiet, Scamper, quiet. You shall join in the excitement in a minute. Listen, all of you. That thief is still somewhere in the woods – maybe in Mr Burton's hut this very minute. I don't believe he has found those hidden valuables – and he won't leave till he does. Well then . . .'

'Well, then, we'd better tell the *police* what we think!' cried Jack. 'Or he may find the hidden goods and disappear. Aren't we idiots not to have thought of it before? All that fuss and excitement over that robbery – and here we've had the third robber hanging about our shed for ages!'

'And we thought it was poor Susie,' said Janet. 'Honestly, I feel awful about that.'

'Look – don't forget it's Bonfire Night,' said Barbara. 'Telephone the police straight away, or we'll never have time to rebuild our bonfire and take the guy out and burn him. *Please* don't let's spoil Bonfire Night.'

'All right, all right,' said Peter. 'I'll go and tell the police what we think – though they may not believe it, of course. Jack, you and George take out the guy. Pam, you're responsible for the fireworks. Janet, remember the matches for the bonfire. Colin and Barbara, start rebuilding it as quickly as you can!'

'Right, Captain!' said Jack. 'Scamper – lead the way!'

'And for goodness' sake look out for the thief!' shouted Peter, as he ran out of the shed door to go in and telephone. 'I bet he's still about somewhere!'

CHAPTER NINETEEN

Quite a lot happens

EVERYONE OBEYED orders, and very soon the guy, in his old raincoat and cap, was being carried out of the shed in his chair, and down the garden into the field. Janet raced up to the house for a box of matches.

Soon they were all in the field. It was getting dark now, and they would have to use their torches before long.

'Bother!' said Jack, feeling a few spots of rain on his face. 'I believe it's going to rain!'

Colin and Barbara set to work to build up the scattered bonfire heap. It wasn't very easy in the half-darkness. Jack and George helped too, once they had set down the guy.

Colin suddenly pulled Janet's coat. 'Hey,' he said, in a whisper. 'Look – is that someone over there – on the other side of the field?'

Janet looked – and what she saw made her nudge Jack and George. 'Be very quiet!' she said, in a low voice. 'Look over there!'

They all looked across the misty, rainy field, and saw what Colin had seen . . . a man, digging, digging, digging! He hadn't seen them away in the distance, for he had his back to them.

'The third robber!' whispered Janet. 'What do we do now?'

'Take no notice at all,' said Colin. 'Just keep him under our eye till the police come. That's about all we can do.'

'Can you see if he's dressed in our guy's old clothes?' whispered Pam.

'No – it's too misty now, and he's just too far away,' said Colin. 'But it *must* be the thief – else why is he digging? Come on. Build up the bonfire. Stick the guy on top. Pretend we're going about our own business and haven't even noticed him.'

So they all rebuilt the bonfire at top speed,

and then, with a great heave, set the guy and his chair firmly on top.

'He's sitting there beautifully,' said Jack. 'Firm as anything. Blow this rain – I don't believe our bonfire will light up at all. Everything's getting soaked.'

'I think it's terribly disappointing,' said Pam. 'Every single thing's gone wrong with our wonderful bonfire plans! Everything!'

'Shut up – the man's coming across the field,' said Colin, in a low voice. 'Don't be afraid –

we've got Scamper. Get on with the bonfire, and talk, and don't take any notice.'

The man was now almost up to them. Pam glanced round and gave a little cry, which she choked in her throat – he was wearing the trousers, the tweed coat, the rubber boots and the cap in which their guy had first been dressed! Scamper had now begun to bark and growl. The man spoke roughly.

'Clear out of this field. It belongs to the farmer. You're not allowed to have bonfires here.'

'My father is the farmer it belongs to,' said

Janet. 'He knows we are building it here. Please be careful of our dog. He bites.'

The man lifted his spade as Scamper jumped round him, barking, and the children all yelled at once.

'Don't you hit him!'

'Stop that!'

'Put that spade down, don't hit the dog!'

'Scamper, come here!'

What would have happened next nobody knew – for quite suddenly two cars drew up on the road side of the field, and six dark figures leapt out.

'The police!' shouted Jack, excited. 'Look – they've come already!'

In a trice the man was off in the rainy mist, with Scamper at his heels and the six children after him. He kicked out at the dog and struck him on the leg. Scamper yelped and came limping back to Janet.

'Here's the man, somewhere over here!' shouted Jack, waving his torch. The dark figures fanned out and came across the field. Then suddenly someone ran panting up to them from behind – and it was Peter, who, after telephoning the police, had stopped to tell everything to his mother, and had then raced down to the field to join the others.

'Gosh – the police have been quick!' he said. 'They believed my story – every word of it! Did I hear you say the man was here in the field?'

'Yes – Scamper went after him and so did we,' said Jack. 'But he kicked him and hurt him. Watch out for the man – but let's keep together. The man ran off over in that direction. He's sure to be caught, the police are all round the field.'

Scamper limped off, barking. *He* had caught sight of the man. It was maddening for the Seven to stand in the half-darkness, and hear shouts, and the sounds of running footsteps, and not be able to see a thing in the rain that was now pouring down.

Scamper gave a yelp as if he was in pain, and the Seven ran to him. Peter felt his leg anxiously. 'I don't *think* it's broken!' he said.

A policeman came up. 'Did you see that fellow on this side of the field?' he said. 'I'm afraid we've lost him in this rain. Good gracious

– whatever's that thing right over there?'

'It's our bonfire,' said Peter. 'And the poor old guy's sitting on top, waiting to be burnt – but he'll be so wet through we'll have to give up all idea of it, I'm afraid.'

'Gave me quite a turn, seeing the guy up there on that heap,' said the policeman. 'Well – I'm afraid we'll have to give up the chase. The man may have slipped into the wood – we'll never get him there.'

The Seven heard the policemen gathering together, and then by the light of their torches making for the two police cars.

'Bother!' said Peter. 'Now that man won't be caught. He may be a mile away by now.'

'He's not,' said Janet, suddenly, right in his ear, in a voice shaking with excitement. 'He's not! Peter – he's sitting up there on our bonfire! He's got the guy's raincoat on – but I saw his rubber boots in the light of my torch. *That's* where he's hiding, Peter! He knew we wouldn't light the bonfire in this rain!'

Peter let out a long breath of amazement, and walked over to the bonfire. Yes – Janet was right! What a hiding-place! There sat the thief, in the guy's chair, the raincoat over his clothes, the mask on his face – on the top of the bonfire! Thrown down behind was the real guy, robbed of his coat and mask.

'Stay here and fiddle about round the bonfire,' Peter said in a low voice to the others. 'I'll take Scamper in case he smells the man up there and barks – and I'll try and catch the police before they drive off. Stay here now, while I rush across the field.'

CHAPTER TWENTY

Bang! Crash! Whoosh!

PETER TORE right across the field. He shouted as he came near the cars, and waved his torch. One car was just driving off, but stopped.

'We've got the man!' he shouted. 'He's sitting on top of our bonfire, dressed in the guy's

raincoat and mask, but we saw his boots. Come quickly.'

Everything then happened very, very suddenly. The police raced across the field, the man leapt off the bonfire, Scamper limped on three legs to stop him – and over went the thief! Before he could get up, he was caught! He began to shout and struggle.

'You go back home, you kids,' said the sergeant. 'You'll get soaked. Sorry your Bonfire Night's been spoilt – you'd better have it tomorrow! We'll be digging up this field in the morning, and maybe we'll get the buried goods before you light your bonfire! We'll come and dance round it if we do!'

The Seven watched the policemen disappear through the rain, the prisoner held tightly. Janet gave an enormous sigh.

'I suddenly feel dreadfully tired,' she said. 'Let's go in. I'm soaked.'

'Well, it was very exciting, but not much of a bonfire night – especially after all our wonderful plans,' said Jack.

'And poor Scamper's hurt,' said Peter. 'I don't feel like having a bonfire night at all, now.

Let's give up the idea – and not bother about it tomorrow. After all, we've not got an enormous lot of fireworks – and our bonfire's soaked – and so is our guy. Come on in.'

But next morning they all felt very differently! The sergeant telephoned to say that they could have the third robber's guy clothes if they wanted them – they had found the man's own clothes. 'And I have another little surprise for you,' he said.

'What?' asked Peter.

'Well, I'm very pleased with your help,' said the sergeant. 'And I am sending along a bumper box of fireworks to Peter's father for your late Bonfire Night party. Enough for about twenty of you. Have a good time tonight but take care not to go too near!'

'Oh – thanks a lot!' said Peter, thrilled.

All the others were delighted too, when they heard, and great plans were made after morning school.

'My mother says you are all to come at five and she'll give us a delicious tea – and Dad will come out and set the bonfire going with us,' said Peter.

274

'And Mr Burton's coming back today and says he'll build the bonfire sky-high,' said Janet. 'The other wood is soaked through. He'll bring some dry branches from the wood-shed.'

'There's just one thing more,' said Peter. 'Jack, I feel *awful* about Susie. Simply awful. I mean – we accused her and the others of – of –'

'Go on – say it – of stealing!' said Jack. 'Well – *they* didn't have any fireworks last night either – I expect you'd like them to come to our show tonight, wouldn't you?'

'Yes. Yes, we'd *all* like them to,' said Peter. 'But do you think Susie will *want* to come? After all, we were pretty beastly in the things we said.'

'Let's write her a note from every one of us,' said Janet. So between them they wrote a note, and Jack gave it to Susie. She looked most astonished and opened it at once.

'*Dear Susie,*' she read,

'*First of all we're very sorry for all the awful things we said. We really are. We would be awfully glad if you and Hilda and Doris would*

275

come to our firework party tonight. There'll be the biggest box of fireworks you ever saw. Please do come and watch as Peter's father sets them off. Come to tea in the shed first. The password is Wee Willie Winkie.

With many apologies to you from

The Secret Seven.'

'Gracious goodness!' said Susie, her eyes shining. 'Wait till Hilda and Doris see this! Come to your *party*? I should jolly well think we will! And *gosh* – does it really mean that we can meet in the shed with you – and say the password?'

'Yes – but only just this *once*,' said Jack. 'And please do behave yourself, Susie, and tell Hilda and Doris to as well.'

'Oh, I *will*,' said Susie. 'Gosh – *what* a surprise!'

And so, for the first time, Susie actually said the password and was admitted to the Secret Seven shed with Hilda and Doris. Not to a *meeting*, though – just to a tea-party. She was really very nice, for she waved away everyone's apologies, and smiled round in delight.

'Don't apologise! I've said just as awful

things as you did, and done them too! We did our best to spoil your bonfire night – though that thief did far more than we did! And thanks *most* awfully for letting us come here and say the password. I never, *never* thought you'd do that.'

Everyone warmed to the generous-natured Susie, and Janet began to wonder however they could have thought such dreadful things of her and the others. 'But oh dear – I wouldn't be surprised if Susie's nice behaviour doesn't last very long,' she thought. 'Or ours either, come to that! So we must make the best of tonight!'

They certainly did. Come out to the field and listen.

BANG! CRASH! WHIZZZZZZZZZ! Who-ooosh-ee-who-ooosh-eewhooosh! Peter's father had let off the first Moon Rocket!

277

Sizzle-sizzle-sizzle – the bonfire is burning high – what a sight the flames are! And there's the old guy, plump and wobbly, dressed in coat, trousers, boots and cap, sitting high on top. Bang! A rocket flew by his ear, and made him jerk his head.

'He's laughing! The old guy's laughing!' shouted Janet, dancing round the bonfire. 'He says he's as warm as toast at last!'

BANG! Goodbye, Secret Seven, see you again soon! WHOOOOOOOSH! That rocket's soared over the trees! CRASH! What in the wide world was that?

Only one figure is missing from the Grand Firework Party. Guess who it is? Yes, it's dear old Scamper. He's terrified of bangs and crashes, so he is lying comfortably in his basket by the fire, pretending that he can't go because his leg is bandaged!

Goodbye, Scamper! Give the Secret Seven a lick from us when next you see them!

It is illegal for fireworks to be sold to children. We recommend that fireworks should always be stored and handled by adults.

Always follow the Firework Safety Code:

1. **Never** play with fireworks. They are explosives and can hurt you.
2. **Only** adults should light or hold fireworks.
3. **When** you are watching fireworks, stand well back.
4. **Never** go near a firework that has been lit. Even if it hasn't gone off, it could still explode.
5. **Fireworks** will frighten your pets, so keep them indoors.
6. If you are given a sparkler:
   Always wear gloves.
   Hold it at arm's length.
   When your sparkler goes out, DON'T TOUCH IT. It could still burn you so put it hot end down in a bucket of water.
   Never give sparklers to a child under five.

Remember you have to be 18 years old before you are allowed to buy fireworks in the shops.

GOOD OLD SECRET SEVEN

Contents

1 A meeting is called   285

2 That awful Susie!   291

3 Jack's present   298

4 The wonderful telescope   304

5 Through the telescope   310

6 A face at the window!   316

7 Susie is very annoying   323

8 Up at the castle   329

9 An exciting time!   335

10 Another meeting   341

11 Susie's tale   348

12 Susie has plenty to say!   355

13 The telescope again   361

14 A horrid shock   367

15 Exciting plans   372

16 After supper   380

17 Up in the castle   387

18 An exciting discovery   394

19 A friend in need!   402

20 Safe home again!   408

CHAPTER ONE

A meeting is called

ONE MORNING after school, Peter went to find his sister Janet.

'Hey, Janet!' he called. 'I'm calling a Secret Seven meeting for tomorrow morning. Jack's uncle has given him a super present, and he wants all the Seven to share it.'

'What is it?' asked Janet. 'A game of some sort?'

'No. You'll have to wait and see,' said Peter. 'It's Jack's surprise, not mine. Will you write out a few notes and tell the others to come – 10 o'clock sharp. Thank goodness it's Saturday tomorrow.'

'Wuff,' said Scamper the spaniel. He loved Saturdays too. He knew he would have Peter and Janet all day long then.

'Yes, *you* shall come to the meeting as well,' said Janet, patting his soft golden coat. 'But do you know the password, Scamper?'

'Wuff-wuff!' said Scamper at once, and the children laughed.

'Quite right – the password *is* "wuff-wuff",' said Peter. 'What a good memory you have, Scamper!'

Scamper wagged his tail, and said 'wuff-wuff' again. 'Better not say it too often, Scamper,' said Janet. 'Or that awful Susie might hear you.'

Susie was Jack's sister, and *not* one of the Secret Seven, though she badly wanted to belong. She loved to find out whatever password the Secret Seven were using, and it really was quite difficult to stop her.

Janet scribbled four cards – one to Colin, one to George, one to Pam and one to Barbara. 'There!' she said, 'I'll take them round on my bike. I don't need to write to Jack, as he's asked for the meeting himself. Is he going to bring this present of his tomorrow, whatever it is?'

'Yes,' said Peter. 'I'd better tidy up the shed where we meet – and I'll ask Mother what she

can spare for us to eat. I *think* she is baking today, so perhaps there'll be something special!'

Next morning Janet and Peter went down to their shed at a quarter to ten, carrying a good many things. 'I've tidied it up,' said Peter. 'The gardener had been in and taken two of the big flower-pots we used as seats, but I found two boxes instead.'

The shed-door had on it the two big letters S.S., standing for Secret Seven. Janet and Peter looked at them proudly.

'Secret Seven!' said Janet. 'Best club in the

world! I *shall* enjoy a meeting again – it's weeks since we had one – we've been so busy with school things.'

In they went, and shut the door. Now no one would be allowed in unless they gave the password. Peter set down the things he was carrying, and looked round proudly. 'Didn't I clean the shed well?' he said. 'I even cleaned the windows. It's nice and warm too, isn't it?'

The shed backed on to the hot greenhouse, and so gained some of the heat from there. It was pleasantly warm on this cold November day. Janet began to set out some coloured mugs, taking them down from the shelf.

'Mother thought we'd better have hot cocoa this cold day,' she said. 'I'll fetch it as soon as everyone is here. I bet Jack will be first with his wonderful present, whatever it is! Where's Scamper?'

'I don't know. He didn't come down with us. I expect he'll turn up,' said Peter. 'He's probably

chasing his old enemy – the stable cat. He *still* thinks he can catch her, though he never will.'

'Look what Mother's given us,' said Janet, showing Peter a tin full of buns. 'Currant buns warm from the oven – and a home-made macaroon for each of us!'

'Good old Mother!' said Peter, sniffing at the warm buns. 'One of these days I'll buy her a medal. Hurry up, Janet – the others will be here in half a minute. I hope they'll all remember the password! Listen – here comes the first one. I bet it's Jack.'

CHAPTER TWO

That awful Susie!

A FIST banged on the door, and Peter called out at once. 'Password, please.'

'Wuff-wuff!' said a voice, rather loudly.

'Enter,' said Peter, 'and DO remember not to say the password so that everyone can hear it for a mile around!'

'Sorry!' said George, coming in at the door, a grin on his face. 'Did I sound like Scamper? I tried to.'

'Well, you didn't,' said Janet. 'You sounded exactly like yourself. Sit down, George. We thought you were Jack. He said he'd be here early, because he has something to show us.'

Knock-knock – somebody else had come.

'Password!' yelled Peter, and the answer came at once. 'Wuff-wuff! Wuff-wuff!'

In came Pam and Barbara, beaming all over their faces. 'Hello! We're not the last. Good!'

Bang-bang! '*That* must be Jack,' said Janet, as Peter called out 'Password, please!' But it wasn't. It was Colin. He marched in and shut the door smartly. 'Hello, everyone! I say, it's nice and warm in here! What's the meeting called for? Anything special?'

'Yes,' said Peter. 'Jack asked me to call it. He has something very interesting to show us. I can't think why he's not here. It's past ten, and he said he'd be early.'

'I bet it's that awful sister of his who's stopping him coming,' said Pam.

'But how could she know about our meeting?' said Peter. 'Jack wouldn't tell her, I'm sure.'

'Here's Jack,' said Barbara, as more footsteps came down the path to the shed. Someone gave the door such a bang that they all jumped. Before Peter could call out 'Password' a voice shouted it loudly. 'WUFF-WUFF.'

'Enter!' cried Peter, sure it was Jack's voice.

The door flew open – and there stood Susie, Jack's sister! She grinned round at them.

'Thanks for inviting me to your meeting,' she said, and shut the door behind her. She sat down on a box before anyone could stop her.

'Susie! How dare you!' shouted Peter and Janet together. Peter threw the door open. 'Go away!' he said. 'You know you've no right here. You don't belong to the Secret Seven.'

'Well, you'd better *let* me belong then,' said Susie. 'Because my mother says that the present Jack had from our Uncle Bob is to be shared between us! And as he's bringing it here to show you today, *I've* come to share it too.'

Someone else came down the path, carrying something over his shoulder – something long and straight. There was a loud knock on the door, and the password was said very clearly.

'Wuff-wuff,' said Jack's voice. It was exactly like Susie's, so no wonder everyone had thought she was Jack!

'Enter!' called Peter. Jack came in, carrying his load carefully. He glared angrily at Susie.

'How did she know our password, Jack?' asked Peter, sternly. 'Did you tell her?'

'No, he didn't. I just hid in a bush outside and listened,' said Susie. 'You needn't glare at me like that, Jack. Mother said I could share that present, you know she did.'

'Can't we turn her out?' said Pam, who didn't like Susie at all. 'She always tries to spoil everything!'

'You just *try* to turn me out!' said Susie, fiercely. 'I don't want to come to your silly old meetings – but I tell you, I'm going to share Jack's present as much as any of *you* are.'

Peter looked at her in despair. What could you do with a girl like Susie? If they tried to turn her out she would probably shout and yell, and bring his mother down to see what was the matter – and Mother might even *agree* that Susie should stay and hear what Jack said about his present.

'Tomorrow Binkie, my friend, is coming to stay with me,' said Susie. 'And I've said *she* can share the present too – my half of it, I mean.'

'*Binkie* – that awful little rabbit-face?' said George, in horror. 'That silly giggler – that . . .'

Everyone groaned. Susie alone was bad enough, but when she and Binkie were together the two girls were impossible.

'Well – what are you going to do?' asked

Susie. 'All rush on me together and throw me out? Or let me stay here at the meeting?'

Peter made up his mind quickly. On NO account could Susie attend one of the Secret Seven meetings. On the other hand they couldn't throw her out. She would make such a fuss! Very well then – he must declare the meeting ended, and say that there would be *no* proper meeting, but just a talk about Jack's present, whatever it was.

'I declare this Secret Seven meeting ended,' he said, in a loud voice. 'We will all go indoors and see Jack's present in our playroom. I will NOT have strangers present at our secret meetings.' He got up, and all the others stood too – except Susie.

'All right, all right – you win,' she said. 'Your mother would be cross with me, I know, if I go indoors with you. She'll think I've interfered. But just you listen for a minute, and hear *my* side of the question!'

CHAPTER THREE

Jack's present

BUT BEFORE Susie could go on, footsteps pattered up to the shed-door, and someone scraped at the bottom. 'Password!' shouted Peter, and a doggy voice answered at once, 'WUFF-WUFF-WUFF!'

'Enter, Scamper,' said Peter. 'But you said

too many wuffs! Clever dog, to remember the password!'

That made them all laugh, even Susie. Scamper trotted in and licked everyone in delight. Then he lay down at Peter's feet, panting. 'You're late, Scamper,' said Peter. 'But it doesn't matter because I've declared the meeting ended. Susie, if you've anything to say, say it, and go.'

'All right,' said Susie. 'That thing Jack has brought is a present from our Uncle Bob, who was once a sailor. It's a telescope – and a really fine one, too!'

'*A telescope!*' said everyone, excited. Yes – now they could see that it was. Jack began to take off the wrappings sulkily, as Susie went on talking.

'Well, Jack's idea was to bring it down here and give it to the Secret Seven,' said Susie. 'But Mother said Uncle Bob meant *me* to share it – and I didn't see why you Secret Seven should have it all. I knew I'd never see it once it was installed in this shed. So I argued with Jack . . .'

'Shouted the place down, you mean!' said poor Jack.

'And Mother heard, and she came, and she said Jack *was* to share the telescope with me, though she was pleased that the Secret Seven could look through it too. And Jack said he didn't care what Mother said, he wasn't going to let me share any of it – so I shot off by myself and came to the meeting to tell you all this.'

'And left me behind with Mother in a real rage,' said Jack. 'I'm so sorry, everyone. I meant to leave the telescope here in the shed, so that we could all use it, and look at all sorts of things in the distance – the different cars going along the hillside road – the castle on the hill – the herons on the old pond – it would have been such fun.'

'Yes – fun for *you* – but not for me!' said Susie. 'And what about Binkie? *You* want to share the telescope with Peter and Janet and the rest, don't you – well, I want to share it with Binkie!'

'I shouldn't think Binkie knows what a telescope *is*!' said Jack. 'Her head's full of wool, not brains! *She* won't want to use a telescope.'

'Now listen,' said Peter, making up his mind

quickly. 'You'll *have* to share with Susie, Jack, if your mother says so. But why shouldn't we keep it down here in the shed, so that *any* of us can use it at any time? Not at a special meeting or anything like that.'

'We'd have to keep the shed locked, then,' said Jack. 'This telescope is quite valuable, Uncle said. But that means that Susie will have to know where the key is!'

'Well – as long as she doesn't try to come to any of our meetings again and spoil them as she has spoilt today's, I don't see why she shouldn't know where the key is,' said Peter. 'We've got to be fair about this, Jack. I bet *my* mother would say I'd got to share with Janet if someone gave me something like this telescope. Let's be fair.'

'All right,' said Jack gloomily. '*Be* fair. But don't blame *me* if Susie and Binkie spy on us and find out all our secrets and passwords and everything.'

'Let's have something to eat and drink,' said Janet. 'We'll all feel better then. You'd better have some too, Susie. Being cross always makes people hungry.'

'Well, I'm *not* hungry,' said Susie, getting up. 'But thank you all the same, Janet. I know when I'm not wanted. I only came to say I'm *going* to share the telescope.'

'Wait a bit,' said Colin, seeing that Susie was near tears, for all her boldness. 'Before you go we'd better arrange where the

key is to be hidden. Then you'll know where to look for it.'

'Tell Jack, and *he* can tell me,' said Susie, stalking out of the door. 'Goodbye, stuck-ups! Wait till I tell Binkie about this!'

She slammed the door so hard that Scamper

jumped and began to bark. Jack looked round at the others, feeling ashamed of his sister.

'Susie's got such a temper,' he said. 'I'm so sorry about this.'

'Let's not talk about Susie,' said Janet. 'She didn't go off because she didn't want to share our food – she went because she was afraid she was going to cry. And I can just imagine how awful she'd feel if she did – in front of all of us!'

So nobody said another word about Susie, but tucked into currant buns and macaroons and hot cocoa. Scamper had his share, and thoroughly enjoyed himself. He went to sniff all round the big, strange-looking parcel that Jack had brought into the shed.

'No one seems interested in my telescope except Scamper,' said Jack, in a forlorn voice. 'And I was so very excited about it.'

Peter clapped him on the shoulder. 'So are we! Come on – let's see this wonderful present!'

CHAPTER FOUR

The wonderful telescope

THE WRAPPINGS were soon off – and the Seven crowded round as Jack put the big telescope together, and showed them how the long tube could be stretched out even longer.

'You've no idea how far the telescope's eye can see,' he said. 'When I looked through it this morning before I came, I could see the scarecrow in the field half a mile from our house – and what is more I could see a sparrow or some bird sitting on his hat!'

'Do let's look through it,' said Janet, excited. 'Let's take it out into the garden, and train it on something far away.'

So they carried it out into the garden, and set it on its little stand on the broad top of the low

garden wall. Jack was very clever at adjusting the lens so that it focused properly, and made everything as clear as could be.

'Now that's exactly right,' said Jack, looking through the telescope. 'I've trained it on that little cottage over on the slope there. Before you look through the telescope tell me what you can see with your bare eyes.'

'Well – the cottage, of course,' said Pam. 'And something in the garden, I can't see what.'

'And somebody on the path. That's about all,' said Barbara.

'Right. Well, look through the telescope and you'll see a whole lot more!' said Jack. 'You first, Peter – you're our leader.'

So Peter looked through the long telescope, and immediately gave a loud cry. 'Jack! It's marvellous! I can see Mrs Haddon as if she was just over our wall – and I can even see the jug she is carrying. And that's a pram in the garden – and I can see the baby's teddy bear sitting up at the end of it! And . . .'

'Let *me* have a turn,' said Janet, itching to have a look. 'Goodness! I can see something

sticking out of the chimney! It must be a chimney sweep's brush. Yes, it is! And there's a cat sitting just inside the window! Oh, Jack – it's as if I've magic eyes that can see for miles! Oh, aren't you lucky to have a telescope like this? What fun we'll have!'

Jack was very pleased at the excitement his telescope caused, as one after another the Secret Seven peered through it. 'We can have great fun with it,' he said, proudly. 'We can watch the birds and see everything they do. We can examine every aeroplane that comes overhead. We can . . .'

'Children! Whatever *are* you doing standing still out in the cold for so long?' suddenly cried a voice. 'You'll get colds, all of you! What's that you've got?'

'It's a telescope, Mother,' called Janet. 'It belongs to Jack. He's sharing it with us.'

'How lovely! But do you know how late it's getting?' called her mother.

'Well, we'll put the telescope away now,' said Jack. 'I'm supposed to get home to an early lunch. Come on – help me with it, Colin.'

Soon the telescope was safely in the shed, wrapped up very carefully.

'It's very good of you to share it with us,' said Peter, 'and to say we can all use it when we like. But I think we'd better say that I or Janet must be told when anyone comes to borrow it – we'll be *responsible* for it, see? Is that understood, everyone?'

'Oh yes! We'll come and tell you when we want to look through it,' said George, and the others agreed. 'But suppose you're out? We'd better know where the key of the shed is to be kept, Peter.'

'Oh – of course,' said Peter. 'Let's think now – somewhere fairly easy to get – but yet well hidden. What about under this flat stone here, just by the shed? Scamper, you're the only one not allowed to touch the stone or the key. Understand?'

'Wuff,' said Scamper solemnly and wagged his tail. He watched while Peter carefully slid the key under the stone.

'I'll have to tell Susie where it is,' said Jack, in rather a small voice.

'I know. We promised that,' said Peter. 'She

will *have* to go into our shed, but we'll be careful not to leave any Secret Seven secrets about! Tell her where the key is – and say she MUST put it back under the stone if she ever uses it.'

'Right,' said Jack. 'Er – what about a new password, Peter? Susie knows our last one.'

'Goodness, yes. I'd forgotten that,' said Peter. 'Well, I think it's quite obvious what we'll have! The next password, members, is – TELESCOPE!'

Then off they all went, and Peter and Janet carried everything carefully back to the house. Scamper followed them, wagging his tail. 'Wuff-wuff!' he said, and Peter laughed. 'No – that's our *old* password, Scamper. You'll have to remember the *new* one!'

CHAPTER FIVE

Through the telescope

THE TELESCOPE was a great success. The Secret Seven found it a most fascinating pastime to peer through it at all kinds of things, and there was much coming and going at the meeting-shed.

'I'm writing an essay on gulls in winter-time,' said George, arriving one dinner hour, complete with sandwiches to eat. 'I thought I'd set up the telescope and watch the gulls on your father's fields, Peter – there are always so many there, at this time of year.'

So there sat George, solemnly chewing ham sandwiches, and peering through the telescope at the excited gulls foraging in a newly ploughed field. No wonder he had ten out of ten for his essay!

Colin wanted to see the big jet-liners that flew steadily on their way overhead. 'I could almost see what the people were having for dinner,' he told an astonished Janet. But she wasn't interested in planes – she loved to swing the telescope round on its stand, and watch the people walking or riding on the distant road.

'It's almost as if they were in the garden,' she said. 'Peter, I saw old Mrs King riding on her tricycle, and I counted the onions in her netbag – twelve she had. And I saw that horrid little Harry Jones ride by the greengrocer's cart and quickly take an orange off it as he went.'

'You'll turn into a peeping Tom if you don't look out,' said Peter. 'I bet young Harry would be horrified if he knew you were watching him across dozens of fields!'

The telescope was used at night too, and the Seven marvelled at the way in which it brought the moon so close to them. They had to take the telescope indoors for that, because Peter's mother said it was too cold to stay outside with it.

Susie came to use it too, of course, with her friend Binkie, who was just as giggly as ever.

They found the key and went into the shed. They took the telescope into the garden and rested it on the wall. Peter saw them there, and went out to them.

'Oooh, run, Susie – here's Peter!' giggled Binkie, pretending to be scared. 'Oh, don't eat us, will you, Peter! Oooh, I'm frightened of you.'

'I only came to see that you knew how to use the telescope,' said Peter, coldly. 'I thought

Susie might want help.'

Susie was busy looking through the telescope. She had it trained on a house some way off – then she swung it to another house. 'There's Mr Roneo painting his greenhouse,' she said. 'The ladder's awfully wobbly. And now I can see Miss Fellows cleaning her window from inside. Now I'm looking at the roof of that big old house – I can see it sticking up above the trees. There's a skylight set in the roof – it's being opened – someone's climbing out! Oh! OH! OH!'

Her sudden loud screaming made Peter jump in fright. 'What's the matter? What's happening?' he demanded. 'Let me see.' But Susie fended Peter off and kept her eye glued to the telescope. 'Someone else has climbed out on the roof now!' she cried. 'And he's chasing the first man. Oh, he's fallen off the roof! Peter, what shall we do? We'd better tell your mother, and get help.'

'Mother's out,' said Peter, worried. 'I'll rush off myself and see what I can do. There's a doctor who lives opposite that old house. I could get him if he's there. What a bit of luck you happened to look through the telescope just then!'

He tore off down the garden – but when he came to the gate, he heard a noise that made him pause. It was the sound of delighted giggling!

He stopped at once – and then strode back angrily. 'What are you laughing at, Binkie? Susie, *did* you really see a man fall off the roof – or not?'

'Well – he might *not* have fallen off,' said Susie. 'I'll look again.' She put her eye to the telescope and peered through it once more. 'I can still see him! He's got his foot caught in the roof gutter now – oh, POOR man, he's hanging upside-down by one foot. Now here comes the other man, he . . .'

'Idiot!' said Peter, angrily. 'All made up, of course! I might easily have gone off to that house and taken the doctor too, and hunted for an imaginary man down in the garden. I suppose you think that's funny?'

'Oh we do, we do!' said Susie, with tears of laughter in her eyes. 'It's *awfully* funny, Peter – you should just have seen your face of horror.

This is a most wonderful telescope. I wonder what I'll see next. *You* have a turn, Binkie, and see if you can spot anything interesting too.'

'You can both clear off,' said Peter, and took firm hold of the telescope. 'If *this* is the kind of thing you're going to use a telescope for, I shall lock it up. GO HOME, BOTH OF YOU!'

And dear me, he looked so fierce, and Scamper began to bark so loudly that Susie and Binkie actually obeyed him, and fled for their lives!

CHAPTER SIX

A face at the window!

IT WASN'T until Janet thought she would turn the telescope on to the big hill where the ruined old castle of Torling stood, that anything really exciting turned up. The castle wasn't much more than a few standing walls, and one great ruined tower in which jackdaws nested.

Janet liked the jackdaws. They sometimes flew down to the farm, and pecked about with the hens, talking all the time in their chattery voices.

'Chack-chack-chack!' they called to one another. Jack and Pam were with Janet the last time she had gone to watch the jackdaws in the fields, and Jack had made them laugh by saying that he kept wanting to say 'Yes, sir!' every time a jackdaw called 'Chack!'

'It sounds exactly as if they're yelling at me,' said Jack, 'just like our games teacher does at football!'

'Chack! Chack!' called a big jackdaw at once, cocking his head on one side and looking up at Jack. 'Chack! Chack!'

'There! He heard what I said,' said Jack, and they all laughed.

The jackdaws nested in the ruins of the old tower, but now that it was November their young ones were grown, and were flying with them. The little colony must have numbered at least a hundred. Janet could see them from her bedroom window, and had often wished the old tower was nearer the farm, so that she could watch the antics of the birds more closely.

'And now I *can*!' she thought. 'We've got that lovely telescope that brings everything so near! Why didn't I think of watching the jackdaws before!'

She went to fetch it, first telling Peter in case he wanted it himself. 'It's really too cold to sit out in the open air with it today,' he said, as he took the key out from under the stone. 'Better take the telescope indoors, Janet. I'll carry it in for you. We could put it up in the boxroom at the top of the house – you'd be out of the way then – and the big window there looks right up the hill to the castle.'

Soon Janet was sitting in the boxroom, surrounded by all kinds of junk, her eye glued to the bottom end of the telescope tube. She had trained it carefully on to the top of the faraway hill, where the jackdaws circled round the tower, a hundred small black dots in the far distance.

But now, seen through the telescope they

became birds, not dots – birds with outspread wings, circling and rising and falling in the misty November day. They played tricks on one another, chased each other, pretended to tumble and then swept away crying 'chack-chack-chack' as if they were laughing. Janet laughed too.

And then she suddenly stiffened on her chair. She was looking at one of the old windows at the top of the tower, through which some of the jackdaws had been flying – but now there were no jackdaws there; they had flown away as if suddenly scared, when something appeared in the window-opening, peeping cautiously over the stone window-ledge.

'What is it?' thought Janet. 'It's not a bird. Surely it can't be a cat? No – it isn't – my goodness me, it's a *head* – a man's head with a hat on – no, a cap. What in the world is he doing?'

The head remained at the window for a few minutes, and then disappeared. Janet knew that there were dangerous, broken steps at one side of the tower, leading almost to the top and she guessed that whoever it was who was there would now be climbing down. She trained the telescope downwards – and caught sight of something moving past one of the lower windows. The man was half-way down!

'Look at that!' she said out loud, astonished. 'Someone's hiding in that old tower! Whatever for? It's ruined and tumble-down and deserted – and dangerous too, because it's gradually subsiding! I must tell Peter!'

She yelled for him and he came up to the boxroom. Janet told him what she had seen, and he too looked through the telescope at the old castle. But he could see nothing moving there, except the jackdaws, who were now once more settling here and there on the castle walls.

'Whoever it was has gone into hiding down below,' said Janet, beginning to feel excited. 'So the jackdaws aren't frightened any longer. Who can it be, Peter?'

'Can't imagine!' said her brother, puzzled. 'Nobody ever goes there in the winter – and anyway, it's supposed to be dangerous now. Some stones fell down this spring, you know – right off the top of the tower! Are you quite

sure you saw a face at the window? Which window was it?'

Janet told him, and Peter gazed at it through the telescope, moving it downwards to other openings. He gave a sudden exclamation.

'Yes! There *is* someone there! I saw something moving down below – on the ground floor. I'm sure someone passed quickly across the doorway, just inside! No wonder the jackdaws keep flying up in fright!'

'We must tell the Secret Seven,' said Janet,

excited. 'You never know, Peter – this might be something mysterious, something that . . .'

Peter laughed. 'It's probably just some tramp looking for shelter! Still, we'll tell the others and see what *they* think!'

CHAPTER SEVEN

Susie is very annoying

NEXT DAY, when Peter walked home with Jack and George after school, he told them what he and Janet had seen through the telescope. 'Janet saw a face – the head of a man wearing a cap,' he said. 'And I distinctly saw someone moving behind the great doorway of the castle. I think there's a man hiding up there.'

'Well, if he were hiding, surely he wouldn't give himself away by peering through windows and walking across open doorways!' objected Jack. 'I expect it was just a chance visitor.'

'Look, Jack – anyone hiding up there would never, never imagine that anybody could *possibly* spot him in the castle, far away from everywhere, at the top of that hill!' said Peter.

'It was only because we were using your powerful telescope that that man was seen! He could never be spotted with the naked eye.'

'Yes – you're right there,' said George. 'I didn't think of that. The castle is so lonely and deserted on the top of that steep hill that anyone might judge it safe to hide there in the wintertime. But it must be so cold! Where does he sleep, do you think?'

'Down in the old dungeons?' suggested Peter, with a shiver. 'Have you ever seen them? You go down about a hundred steps into a cold, dark, echoing place – rather like a most *enormous* cellar! Hundreds of years ago prisoners were kept down there.'

'How horrible people must have been in those days!' said George. 'I couldn't even keep a dog or cat down in a cellar!'

'What about us going up to the old castle and having a snoop round?' said Jack. 'I've never been there.'

'Well, it's rather dangerous now, my dad says,' said George. 'But the dangerous places have warning notices up, so I dare say we'd be all right. After all, we're pretty sensible, or Peter wouldn't allow us to belong to the Secret Seven!'

That made the others laugh. 'Quite right,' said Peter. 'No idiots allowed in the S.S. Club! Well, what about it – *shall* we go up to the castle? We could bike or walk, whichever you like.'

'Bike,' said Jack. 'It's true we'll have to walk up most of the castle hill, it's so steep – but it will be fun to coast down.'

'Right. Saturday morning, then,' said Peter. 'We'll ask Colin if he'd like to come, but not the girls – the hill would be a bit steep for them.'

But the three girls had quite other ideas about that. 'Too steep indeed!' snorted Janet, when Peter told her what he and the other boys had planned. 'I bet I could ride right up that hill and get to the top before you did! We're *all* coming, see? Pam and Barbara, too. This is a Secret Seven thing, and we'll all be in it. Anyway, *I* discovered there was someone hiding in thc castle, not you!'

'All right, all right, all *right*,' said Peter, backing away. 'Don't bite my nose off. I'll ring up Jack and tell him it's to be a Secret Seven outing. We'll all wear our badges.'

So he rang up Jack, and told him that Janet insisted on the three girls coming.

'What a nuisance!' said Jack. 'It's quite a way to the castle – and we'll have to bike slowly or the girls won't keep up with us.'

'What's this you're phoning about?' said Susie, suddenly appearing at the door of the room in which Jack was phoning. 'Are you going on a spree or something? I'd like to come too. It would be a treat for Binkie.'

'Well, you're *not* coming!' said Jack. 'It's a Secret Seven outing. And do shut up a minute. Can't you see I'm phoning?' He turned back to the telephone. 'Sorry, Peter. Susie came barging in just then. She said *she* wanted to come too, with Binkie!'

'What a truly horrible idea!' said Peter into the phone. 'They can't, of course. I won't have them.'

'Have you spotted that man again, hiding in the castle?' asked Jack, thinking that Susie had gone out of the room.

'Don't talk about that on the phone,' said Peter, quite cross. 'Anyone might hear! It's *our* secret!'

'Sorry,' said Jack, humbly. 'All right, then – we all of us meet at a quarter to ten, Saturday morning, outside your front gate. Is Scamper coming?'

'No. Too long a run for him,' said Peter. 'Goodbye for now!'

Susie pounced on Jack as soon as he had finished. She had been hiding behind an armchair, listening! Jack glared at her in rage.

'You've been *listening*! Well, a fat lot of good it will do you!' And he stalked out of the room.

'Who's hiding in the old castle? And why are they there, do you think?' asked Susie, following Jack out of the room. 'Go on – tell me. How do you *know* anyone's there? It's too far to see people in the castle. I don't believe it!'

'You forget that we have a telescope, Miss Clever!' said Jack, coldly, and ran up the stairs. Susie made a rude face behind his back.

'Well, *we're* coming too, Binkie and I,' she said. 'We'll be the Secret Nine, instead of the Secret Seven! So there!'

CHAPTER EIGHT

Up at the castle

JACK KNEW perfectly well that Susie would keep her word, and that she and Binkie would follow the Seven on their journey to the old castle. He kicked himself for not having made certain that his annoying sister was out of the room before he finished phoning. He would remember to search thoroughly in future.

With a sigh he went to see Peter, not daring to telephone him again, in case Susie was about. He told him of Susie's threat.

'Well – fancy letting out what our plans were, with *Susie* in the room!' said Peter, in disgust. 'You really *are* a fool! Never mind. We'll simply start half an hour later – but for goodness' *sake* don't let her guess that!'

So, at quarter past ten on Saturday morning, the Secret Seven assembled outside Peter's front gate. All of them had their bicycles with them, and in the baskets were bottles of lemonade, and biscuits. This was Janet's idea, and everyone thought it a very good one.

Jack was the last to arrive, and he pedalled up in a hurry. 'Sorry I'm late,' he said. 'I had to make sure that Susie and Binkie weren't lying in wait somewhere, meaning to come with me!'

'Where are they?' demanded Peter.

'I don't know. But their bikes are still in the shed, so we're safe,' said Jack, thankfully. 'I asked Mother where they were, and she said she heard them talking about going shopping – so *that's* all right!'

'All the same – we'll keep a look-out till we're safely on the way,' said Peter. 'I will *not* have those two messing up our plans.'

They saw no sign whatever of Susie or Binkie and soon forgot about them. After all, if their bikes were in the shed, they couldn't go far!

When they came to the steep road that wound up round the castle hill, they panted and

puffed – and one by one leapt off to walk. It really was *too* steep to ride up. The road did not go to the castle, but passed by it some way off. A footpath over a stile led to the old ruin, and when they came to this the Seven piled their bicycles on top of one another in the hedge, and were soon over the stile. They carried their lemonade and biscuits with them, planning to eat and drink in the shelter of the castle.

It was still some way off up the hill. They all kept a sharp look-out for signs of anyone looking out of the windows, but could see nothing at all.

The jackdaws circled overhead all the time, calling loudly, disturbed at seeing so many children. 'Chack, chack!' they called. 'Chack, chack!'

And Jack answered at once. 'Glad you know me! How are you all?'

'Idiot!' said Peter, laughing. 'Wow – what an enormous number there are! Now, what shall we do first? Look round the old place – go down into the dungeons and snoop around? Eat our biscuits?'

'Let's go inside and eat there,' said Barbara. 'The wind's very strong out here, and I'm cold. I'm hungry, too. We can snoop round afterwards.'

So they all trooped up the broken steps, and in at the great entrance to the castle, where once enormous gates had hung. They stopped in the vast hall inside, and stared in surprise. It was piled high at one side with twigs of all kinds and sizes!

'Who put those here?' said Jack, puzzled. 'Oh, of course – the jackdaws! They nest in the

tower chimney, and
these twigs must have
fallen down from their
nests for years and
years!'

They looked up the
tower. They could see
the sky through a square
hole at the top where
smoke once rose from
the enormous stone
fireplace far below, in
the hall. This was almost
completely hidden by
the fallen twigs, which
had spread out on to the
hall floor as well. They
cracked loudly as the
children trod on them.

A big wooden notice, with DANGER painted
on it, was placed further down the hall, in a
carved stone doorway. The children peered
through it, and saw a big room, with one wall
crumbling dangerously. It looked as if it might
fall at any time.

'We can't go in *there*,' said Peter, at once. 'I shouldn't think anyone would hide in *that* room – I imagine it would be a pretty dangerous hiding-place!'

'Sh!' said Janet, in a low voice. 'Don't talk about hiding-places – if anyone *is* hiding here, they'll hear you.'

'You're right,' said Peter. 'Let's go further down the hall – we'll find plenty more old rooms, I expect, all crumbling away! Come on – and look out for any signs of people hiding!' he added, in a whisper. 'Follow me!'

CHAPTER NINE

An exciting time!

IT WASN'T until they came to what seemed to be a dark kitchen-like place, with a huge stone sink in one corner, that they found anything at all exciting. Jack suddenly stopped and pointed.

The others looked, and saw what appeared to have been a fire, made of sticks, half-burnt

through. Pam gave a little cry as she bent over them.

'Hey – the sticks are still warm! It's not long since this fire was lit!'

'Sh!' said everyone, looking over their shoulders, feeling that whoever had lit that fire might still be about.

Peter felt the twigs. Yes, they were certainly still warm – and what was more, it looked as if someone had stamped out the little fire in a hurry, for it was curiously flattened!

'Talk in loud voices about ordinary things,' commanded Peter, in a whisper. 'And keep your eyes open.'

They followed Peter up some steps to a stone bench in a crumbling recess in the wall. A newspaper had been left there, and they pounced on it.

'What date is it? It might tell us whether anyone has been here recently,' said Colin. He shook it open.

'No – no use,' he said. 'Look – it's dated 16th September – ages ago!'

'Left by some visitor, probably – maybe trippers were still visiting the castle then,' said

Peter. 'Come on – let's have another look round.'

To their great disappointment they could find nothing of any use at all. A few cigarette ends – one or two dead matches – a paper bag that had once held sweets. 'No – I can't say that these are any help,' said Peter.

'I vote we sit down and have our biscuits,' said George, at last, tired of hunting in every corner. 'I'm filthy dirty – just look at my hands!'

'Hey – do you suppose these steps go down to the dungeons?' called Barbara. Everyone turned to see where she was. She stood below a big hand-printed notice. It said: 'THE DUNGEONS. UNSAFE. DESCENT FORBIDDEN.'

'Yes. Look at the notice, idiot,' said Peter. 'Well – we don't go down those steps, that's certain! I don't particularly want an old wall to fall on top of me!'

'Let's have our biscuits sitting on the old stone bench here,' said Jack. 'It will just about take us all. What a castle! The things that must have happened here!'

They all sat down, crowding on to the uneven

old seat. It felt very cold and hard! Soon they were munching their biscuits, and drinking their lemonade out of the little bottles.

'Do you really think anyone's here besides us – hiding somewhere?' said Pam, in a whisper.

'Quite likely,' answered Peter, also in a whisper. 'Probably down in the dungeons! Nobody in their senses would go down there, with that danger notice up!'

'I don't like to think of someone hiding down in that horrible dark dungeon,' said Barbara, a picture of a dreadful damp, smelly, black place coming into her mind. 'I do hope to goodness we don't hear any noises coming from there.'

'Don't be a silly fool,' said George. 'Nobody's down there – why should . . .'

He stopped very suddenly, as a curious noise suddenly came to his ears. Everyone heard it, and stiffened in fright.

It sounded a little like a very unhappy owl. 'Ooooo!' it wailed. 'Ooo-oo-OOOOOOO!'

Pam clutched Barbara and made her jump. 'What is it? Did you hear?'

'Shut up,' said Peter, sharply. 'Listen, everyone. Someone's down in those dungeons.'

'Oooh-ah-oooh-eeeee!' wailed the voice.

Pam gave such a shriek that everyone leapt to their feet. She tumbled down from the seat and ran howling down the stone passage to the hall.

Jack went after her, and the others were just collecting their bags and bottles when another noise made them jump. It, too, came from the dungeons.

'Bang! Bang-bang! Bang!'

'Quick — run!' shouted Peter, clutching Janet,

and pushing her in front of him. 'Back to our bikes!'

'Is that someone shooting?' asked Barbara, fearfully, as they ran, hearing a few more 'bangs' coming from the dungeons.

'Goodness knows!' said Peter. 'Gosh, look how scared the jackdaws are now – and what a row they are making! Whatever can be going on in that castle?'

CHAPTER TEN

Another meeting

WHEN THEY had reached their bicycles safely, they paused to put their bags and bottles into the baskets. Peter was beginning to feel a bit ashamed of their hurried flight.

'Do you think we boys ought to go back and find out what those bangs were?' he said. 'I mean – I don't *think* they were gun-shots, you know – they weren't loud enough.'

'You go if you want to. *I'm* not rushing into danger,' said Colin. 'Something's certainly going on there. Tell the police if you like – and leave *them* to deal with it. What with that half-warm, stamped-out fire of twigs – and those howls and bangs – it's enough to scare grown-ups, let alone *us*!'

'Let's have a meeting about it!' said George. 'We ought to decide what we're going to do. We *know* there's somebody there – so why is he hiding? And what's he doing down in the dungeons, popping away like that? Is he trying to scare us off? Has he something to hide?'

'Let's have a meeting as soon as we get back,' said Janet.

'I can't. I've a music lesson at quarter past twelve,' said Pam. 'Please, *please* don't have a meeting without me.'

'Well, three o'clock this afternoon, then,' said Peter. 'And mind you remember the password – telescope – and wear your badges.'

'*I* can't come then,' said Jack, 'and neither can George. We've got football practice. Make it tomorrow evening.'

'All right. Tomorrow evening then – six o'clock – and be punctual,' said Peter. 'And if I've got time I'll take a look at that castle through the telescope this afternoon. There really *is* something going on there!'

They rode home rather gloomily, all the boys now wishing they had gone into the dungeons – or at least peeped down – to see what was going on. 'Still, we hadn't any torches,' said Peter. 'We couldn't have seen a thing. It sounded very much like owls, didn't it, but it couldn't have been. Owls hoot but they don't make bang-bang noises!'

Jack rode home, hoping that Susie and Binkie were out still and wouldn't ask him questions about his morning. He peeped into the shed and saw that the girls' bikes were still there. Good! They must still be out doing their Saturday shopping!

As soon as Peter was home, he fetched the telescope from the shed, while a delighted Scamper danced round him. The spaniel had not been at all pleased at being left behind that morning, and had lain by the fire, sulking – but now he was so glad to see Peter and Janet again that he could hardly keep still!

Peter took the telescope to the boxroom and set it up. Scamper sniffed at the bottom end with much interest.

'You look up it with your eye, not your *nose*,' said Peter. He set his right eye to the telescope, and trained it on the castle – goodness, was that someone standing in the great doorway?

But before he could see properly, Scamper jumped up to lick him – and over went the telescope! 'Idiot!' said Peter, crossly, and hurriedly picked it up. It seemed quite all right. He set it up again and peered through it excitedly.

But now the doorway was empty. No one stood there. Peter felt really vexed. 'Couldn't you have waited a bit to lick me?' he said to Scamper. 'Oh goodness – now there's *Mother* calling me – and by the time I get back to the boxroom, it'll be too late to spot whoever it was!'

His mother kept him busy for the rest of the morning, and in the afternoon he had to do his homework. He longed to go up and look through the telescope. So did Janet.

There was nothing interesting to be seen when at last they managed to peer through it. In disappointment they took it down to the shed again, and locked it there as usual.

'Cheer up, Peter,' said Janet. 'We're having a meeting tomorrow night, and I've a box of toffees! It will be fun to talk about our morning at the castle.'

On Sunday evening everyone arrived quite punctually, and the password was rattled out five times. 'Telescope!' As George said, it would be easier to remember *that* password than forget it!

They settled down in the warm shed, all seven of them. Peter glanced round to see if they were wearing their badges. Yes – everyone had the S.S. on their coats. Janet handed round the toffees, and they began to talk about the previous morning.

'Someone's hiding at the castle, for *some* reason, that's certain,' began Peter. 'And that someone doesn't want anyone else to know he's there – and scared us away. I feel silly now – I'm sure the man who's hiding there knew we were kids and would run for our lives if he made scary noises!'

'Yes. I've been thinking that too,' said Jack.

'Oh, but they sounded so *awful*,' said Pam, and she gave a little shudder. 'I wouldn't go there again if you gave me a thousand pounds.'

'Well, we're not offering you anything like that,' said Peter. 'So stop shuddering, and talk sense. I think now that we were rather cowardly.'

'But those *bangs*!' said Barbara. 'They sounded so loud and frightening. And those moans and howls!'

'Now let's be sensible,' said Peter. 'I don't suppose . . .'

And then he stopped very suddenly indeed, for from outside the shed came two or three mournful yowls exactly like those the Seven had heard yesterday morning! 'Ooo-oo-OOOO!'

Everyone jumped violently, and Scamper barked and ran to the door, scratching it angrily. There was a dead silence in the shed, except for Scamper. The moaning suddenly stopped.

Then the bangs began! Pop! Pop-pop! POP!

'I'm scared,' whispered Pam, and clutched at Barbara, making her jump.

'Ooo-ooo! Pop-bang-pop!'

Then came a most familiar sound – a giggle, hastily stopped midway. Jack and Peter gave cries of fury and rushed to the door.

'SUSIE! BINKIE! YOU BEASTS!'

The door was flung open so suddenly that the two giggling girls outside were taken by surprise. Jack leapt out and caught Susie. Binkie ran, but came back to help Susie and was caught too. They were both dragged into the shed and set down with a bump on two boxes.

'And now will you just tell us the *meaning* of all this!' said Peter, so angry that he could hardly get the words out of his mouth.

CHAPTER ELEVEN

Susie's tale

'I SHAN'T SAY a word if you shout at me,' said
Susie. 'And Binkie and I will yell the place
down if you're unkind to us.'

'Unkind! UNKIND! Well, what about you and
Binkie!' cried Janet. 'Interfering in all our plans!
It was *you* down in that dungeon, wasn't it –
yowling and – and – well, what *were* you doing
to make those bangs?'

'They weren't bangs – they were loud pops,'
said Susie, with a sudden giggle. 'The same as
we made down in that dungeon. Look – I'll
show you!' The two girls looked highly pleased
with themselves.

And to the great disgust of the Secret Seven
she took a small bundle of coloured rubber out

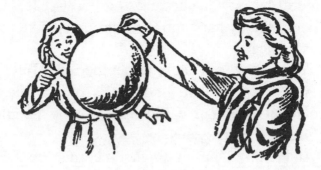

of her pocket and blew hard into it. It swelled up into a truly colossal balloon! Susie held it away from her and Binkie promptly jabbed it with a large pin. POP!

'*That's* what scared you away – balloons popping – and yowls!' said Binkie, giving them a wicked grin, and putting the big pin back under her coat lapel. 'Did our hoots and yowls sound awful coming up those old stone steps?'

'You'd no right to go down into those dungeons,' said Peter, severely. 'Didn't you see the notice? Don't tell me *you* put that notice there!'

'No, we didn't. But it wasn't there when I went up to see the castle with some friends in the summer,' said Binkie, 'so I guessed it couldn't be *very* dangerous to go down! It was only printed by hand too – not properly, like the other notices.'

'So it was,' said Jack, remembering. 'Hey – do you suppose that whoever is hiding there wrote out that notice himself, to stop people prying in the dungeons?'

'And stop them finding something he had hidden there!' exclaimed George. 'It's just like Susie to disobey warnings.'

'*Did* you see anything hidden there?' said Peter. 'Tell us at once.'

'Yes, we did,' said Susie. 'But unless you ask me politely, I shan't tell you anything.'

Peter glared at her. Exasperating, irritating girl! She grinned cheekily at him. 'Say "please, Susie",' she said.

And poor Peter had to do as he was told! He just *had* to know what was down in the dungeons.

'Please, Susie,' he said, quite fiercely.

'Not like that. Really *politely*,' said Susie.

'Susie! I'll shake you to bits if you go on like this!' said Jack suddenly. 'I'm ashamed of you – talking to Peter like that. I'll – I'll . . .'

350

'All right, all right. I'll tell you what we saw,' said Susie, hastily, knowing quite well that her brother would certainly give her a really good shaking if she was cheeky much longer. 'Listen, all of you.'

Everyone listened intently as Susie told what had happened to her and Binkie yesterday morning. Binkie sat beside her, nodding her head every now and then as Susie related her story.

'Well,' began Susie, 'we knew you were all going up there, of course, and we knew you thought there was someone hiding in the castle, because we heard what Jack said on the phone. So we thought we'd go too, and get there *before* you,

so that we could play a few tricks.'

'Yes – but how did you get there? Your bikes were in the shed. I saw them,' said Jack.

'Have you forgotten that there are such things as buses?' said Susie. 'We just caught the bus that goes up the hill and stops at the top. We hopped off and made our way over the fields to the castle – to the *back* of it, not the front, in case you came early.'

'*Buses!* Why didn't we think of that!' groaned Jack. 'So you were there a long time before us?'

'Oh yes – and when we came up to the back of the castle, very quietly, just in *case* anyone was there, we saw someone sitting on an old stone, painting the castle.'

'Painting a *picture* of it, she means,' put in Binkie, seeing that some of the Seven looked rather astonished. 'Goodness – she jumped like anything when we came up behind her, because she hadn't heard us coming over the grass.'

'Did you talk to her?' asked Peter. '*We* thought it was a man there, not a woman. The person I saw through the telescope seemed to have a man's cap on.'

'Oh, this woman had no cap – but she wears her hair sort of piled up on top of her head. I suppose it looked like a cap, in the distance,' said Susie, who was now enjoying herself thoroughly. 'Well . . .'

Scamper suddenly growled and ran to the door. 'Someone's coming!' said Peter. 'Who is it?'

There was a knock at the door, and then came his mother's cheerful voice. 'I won't come in, I know you're talking secrets – but I'm leaving a plate of jam-tarts out here. Seven – is that right?'

'No, nine – ten, counting Scamper!' called Susie, cheekily, before anyone else could say a word. 'It's a Secret *Nine* Meeting tonight!'

'Well, one of you must come and fetch two more then,' she replied, and off she went back to the house.

'Secret *Nine* indeed!' said Janet, very cross. She frowned angrily at Susie. 'You certainly *won't* get any tarts!'

'Right. We'll say goodbye and go home then,' said Susie. 'Come on, Binkie!' And the two of them got up and went to the door!

CHAPTER TWELVE

Susie has plenty to say!

PETER GROANED. He knew when he was beaten! 'All right – you win!' he said. 'Come back and sit down. Colin, go and get three more jam-tarts – old Scamper can have one then.'

Colin departed, with Scamper at his heels. The rest of the Seven sat and looked at Susie in

disgust. What a girl! She smiled cheekily all round. This certainly was Her Evening! Aha! She was teaching those stuck-up Seven a lesson!

Colin came back at once with the tarts, and they all began to eat them, Scamper too.

'Well, about this artist woman,' said Susie, with her mouth full. 'She said we'd better not go into the castle because it was dangerous, so we thanked her for her warning – but, of course, we meant to go without her seeing us!'

'You *would*!' said Jack.

'We stopped and talked a bit, just to see if she had anything interesting to say,' said Susie. 'But she hadn't, really. She just said she loved the old castle, and was painting it, hoping to sell the picture. She said she kept her paints and things inside, because nobody ever came in the winter, so they were quite safe.'

'This looks as if all our suspicions were silly,' said Peter, feeling rather small.

'She was awfully interested in us, too,' went on Susie. 'Wasn't she, Binkie?'

'Oh yes – she asked us a lot of questions –

and she laughed like anything when Susie said Jack and the others were coming up to hunt a man hiding in the castle.'

'You told her *that*!' cried Peter, angrily. 'How dare you? You'd no right to give our plans away.'

'Well, they were silly plans, so it didn't really matter,' said Susie. 'She asked me how in the world you could see anyone in the castle from this farm – we told her you lived here, Peter – and she was *very* interested to hear about the telescope we keep down in this shed, and how easily we could see the castle with it.'

'Susie! You surely didn't give that away too – how *could* you? Now she'll know we're watching what's happening,' groaned Peter. 'Honestly, you must be a nitwit to jabber like that to a stranger.'

'And *you* must be a nitwit to think anything peculiar is going on up at the castle,' said Susie. 'Just a woman artist painting a picture! *No* one's hiding there. She said that she goes down to sleep in the village on the other side of the castle each night – and except for us, not a soul has been to the castle since she came. Ha ha – what about your mystery now?'

The Secret Seven felt very small indeed – and very angry. It had all been so exciting – and now Susie had interfered, and there was nothing left!

'Did you see anything at all in the dungeons?' asked Peter, after a pause.

'Only things that I suppose belonged to the artist,' said Susie. 'Let's see – what was there, Binkie?'

'Pictures,' said Binkie. 'Pictures without

frames. Rather dark and ugly, *I* thought. I suppose the artist had painted them. They were all covered up, of course. We just peeped at them. There was a pile of rugs too, and some tins.'

'The artist said she'd take another day or two to finish the picture, and when it rained she went into the castle for shelter,' said Susie. 'That's how it was you saw her peeping out of that window, I expect. She has all her meals there too, except breakfast and supper. She just opens a tin.'

'Funny sort of life,' said George. 'Well – that's that! If only we'd gone behind the castle *we'd* have seen her too. We just went straight in at the front. You were watching out for us, I suppose, and shot down into the cellar to blow up your stupid balloons.'

'We nearly died of laughing when we heard you yelling with fright, and listened to you racing out of the castle,' said Binkie, and went off into one of her giggling fits.

'Oh do shut up,' said Jack, tired of both Binkie and Susie. 'Go home. Get out of our sight.'

'We thought we'd like to use the telescope, if you don't mind,' said Susie, putting on a most polite voice. 'The moon's rather good tonight.'

'No. This meeting is ending,' said Peter, firmly. 'Scoot, you two girls. I think your behaviour was *disgraceful*.'

'You sound like Miss Cummings, our teacher,' said Susie, in delight. 'Do say all that again!'

'Oh clear out!' said Peter, at the end of his patience. 'And don't *attempt* to do anything funny with our telescope tonight. I forbid you to!'

'But it doesn't belong to *you*,' said Susie, flaring up at once. 'It's half mine. I only *let* you use my half-share in it, I . . .'

'Susie! Be quiet, and come home with me,' said Jack, and he took his sister's arm very firmly indeed. 'I'm ashamed of you!'

He dragged her out of the shed, and Binkie followed. Peter heaved a sigh of relief.

'Thank goodness we've got rid of them! *What* a pair! Well, let's hope that's the last we'll hear of them for some time!'

CHAPTER THIRTEEN

The telescope again

SUSIE AND Binkie were angry with Jack for hauling them away. 'We wanted to look through the telescope again,' complained Susie.

'No, you didn't – you were just being annoying,' said Jack, fiercely.

'Let go of my arm,' said Susie. 'I want to walk by myself.'

'Well, just behave yourself then,' said Jack, quite relieved to let such a wriggler go. The two girls darted off at once, and Jack saw them racing up the road towards home. He heaved a sigh of relief. What COULD anyone do with a sister like Susie?

But Susie and Binkie didn't go home. No –

Susie was quite determined to have her way and take out the telescope that night. She didn't really want to – it was just obstinacy. She had asked for it – had been refused – and that had made her determined to get her own way. Just like Susie!

So, instead of going round the corner and home, the two girls slipped into a gateway, waited till Jack had gone plodding past, and then raced back to Peter's again. They were puffing and panting so much that they hadn't enough breath left to giggle. But they were very thrilled to think they had outwitted poor Jack, who would be almost home by now. Ha! Ha!

In a trice they were down at the shed. It was in darkness now, and well and truly locked. The girls found the key under the stone, and unlocked the wooden door.

They each had a torch, and it was not difficult to set up the telescope on the low garden wall as usual.

'We'll just have a quick look at the moon, so that we can say we saw it through the telescope,' said Susie. 'And then we'll put it

away. Won't the Secret Seven be wild to think we got our way after all!'

They were soon looking through the long tube of the big telescope. The moon was not at all obliging, and stayed behind clouds, so that the night was dark, instead of light.

'Swing the telescope round a bit and look at the old castle,' suggested Binkie. 'Then we can say we saw that too.'

So Susie trained the telescope on to the castle, far away on its steep hill. It was just a great dark shadow in the night, only visible because of the light from the half-hidden moon.

'There,' said Susie, 'now we can . . . oooh – hey – Binkie, there's a *light* in the castle!'

'In the *castle*! What do you mean? Let *me* see!' said Binkie, and glued her eye to the bottom of the telescope. 'Yes! There *is* a light. It's somewhere on the ground floor – is it shining out of the entrance?'

'I don't know. Might be one of the downstairs windows,' said Susie, pushing Binkie aside. 'Yes, there it is – quite clear! What does that mean, do you suppose? That woman said she never slept in the castle – she went down to her lodgings for tea and stayed there! It's a signal to someone, I should think. Yes – that must be it. Perhaps there *is* something going on, after all!'

'Goodness! Let's go and tell Peter then,' said Binkie, excited. 'Or shall we keep it to ourselves?'

'No – we'll tell Peter,' said Susie. 'He'll be *furious* to think we've discovered something else! Come on!' So off they went to find Peter and Janet. They were up in their playroom, doing jigsaws, and were really amazed to see Binkie and Susie again!

'Look here!' began Peter angrily, but Susie stopped him.

'We've got news!' she said. 'There's someone up at the castle, signalling with a light! We saw it! We looked through the telescope. Come and see.'

But Peter only laughed, and sat down to his jigsaw again. '*Another* of your silly jokes,' he said. 'I wonder you're not tired of them. If you think we're going to be taken in again, you're mistaken. Now, if you don't clear out and *keep* out, I'll call Mother. We've had enough of you both for tonight.'

'But, Peter – we looked through the . . .' began Binkie, and was promptly pushed out of the room by Peter and Janet, and Susie was hustled off too. The playroom door banged, and the two girls heard the key being turned in the lock.

'All right! You'll be sorry!' shouted Susie. 'You'll be VERY sorry tomorrow that you didn't listen to us!'

And down the stairs they went, almost crying

with rage. There *was* someone signalling in that castle, there *was*!

CHAPTER FOURTEEN

A horrid shock

NEXT MORNING Janet and Peter went down to their shed after breakfast to clear up the things left there the evening before.

'We've twenty minutes before we need to start for school,' said Peter, looking for the key under the stone. 'Hallo – the key's not here! What's happened to it? I know I put it there last night.'

'Susie must have taken it!' said Janet, frowning. 'Just to spite us. The little nuisance!'

They went to the shed-door to see if Susie had torn off the green letters S.S. that were always there. Good – they were still there – but as they turned away from the shed, Janet gave a cry of surprise.

'Peter! The key's in the *lock*! Susie forgot to

hide it – the idiot! Anyone might break into the shed and take things if it isn't locked.'

They went in, feeling cross. Everything seemed all right – and then Janet frowned. Something was missing, surely? What was it?

'The *telescope*!' she cried suddenly. 'Peter – where's the telescope? It's gone!'

'Susie's taken it!' said Peter, so angry that he stammered over the words. 'Just because I said she wasn't to use it, and because we wouldn't believe her silly story last night about someone signalling in the castle! I'm going to telephone Jack.'

Jack was horrified when he heard Peter's news. He fetched Susie at once.

'You just go to the phone and tell Peter where you've hidden the telescope!' he said. 'It's not in the shed.'

'But we put it back safely,' said Susie, sounding so amazed that Jack felt she must be speaking the truth. 'We did, really.'

'Did you lock the door?' said Jack. Susie looked at Binkie – and then she went very red.

'Oh, Jack – no, I don't think I did. I was so cross because Peter wouldn't believe me, that I just shoved the telescope into the shed, slammed the door – and ran off with Binkie. I can't remember locking it, or hiding the key.'

'We forgot,' said Binkie, in a very small voice. 'Yes, we forgot. Oh that lovely telescope, Jack! Has it been stolen?'

'I expect so,' said Jack, going back to the telephone. 'Of all the idiots! One of these days, Susie, you'll get into serious trouble. It's just as well it's *our* telescope, not anyone else's.'

He told Peter that Susie and Binkie *had* put back the telescope, but had forgotten to lock the door. Peter was very angry. 'So any prying thief snooping round the shed at night could get in,' he said. 'And of course he'd take the telescope – it would be the most valuable thing there! I'll have to tell my dad, Jack.'

'Oh not just yet!' begged Jack. 'Susie would get into such trouble. I know she's an awful girl, but she *is* my sister, and – well – you know how I feel.'

'Right, Jack. We'll wait till tonight, and see if anything turns up,' said Peter. 'Better have a meeting – half-past five, sharp. But DON'T tell Susie.'

'I won't. But she's so worried and upset that I really don't think she'd even *think* of trying any tricks!' said poor Jack. 'I'm awfully worried too. I know it looks as if Susie and Binkie took the telescope themselves, out of spite – but Susie doesn't tell lies, you know, however annoying she is in other ways.'

'I know she doesn't,' said Peter. 'All right. Five-thirty tonight. I'll tell the others.'

So at half-past five that night a rather subdued Seven met once more down in the old shed. Scamper couldn't *think* what was the matter with them, and ran about wagging his tail and trying to cheer them up.

It was a very serious meeting. Everyone already knew about the telescope, because Janet had told the girls in break at school, and Jack and Peter had told George and Colin. Now – what was to be done?

CHAPTER FIFTEEN

Exciting plans

'JACK – YOU'D better say a few words to everyone about Susie,' said Peter.

So Jack explained how Susie had forgotten to lock the door, and was very, very sorry, and asked the Seven to forgive her and Binkie. 'She says they'll do ANYTHING to help us get it back,' finished Jack. 'I'm most terribly sorry myself – and so thankful that it belonged to me and Susie. I'd have felt dreadful if it had belonged to anyone else.' He felt pretty dreadful now, but *that* would have been just *awful*.

'We're sorry too, Jack,' said Peter. 'And we do believe you when you say that Susie *didn't* take the telescope.'

'I think we ought also to believe her tale of the light that she said she and Binkie saw in the castle last night, when they looked through the telescope,' said Jack, earnestly. 'I know Susie is really most annoying, but *honestly*, Secret Seven, I have never, never once known Susie to tell a lie. She plays jokes, I know, and makes us believe silly things – but she never tells a thumping fib – and if she says she saw a light in the castle last night, then she *did*.'

'I see,' said Peter. 'Well, what do the others say? Do we believe it or not?'

'*I* believe it,' said Pam. 'Susie's an idiot and a nuisance, but I've never known her to tell even a small fib at school to get herself out of trouble. She's too proud to do that. She'd rather take her punishment.'

'Susie's very strong really,' said Barbara, which made everyone look scornfully at her. 'Well, you know what I mean,' she went on. 'She's brave – and bold, and don't-care-ish – and she doesn't cry if she hurts herself, and she'll stick by her friends through thick and thin. In some ways I do admire her, but at times she's just a nuisance.'

This rather remarkable speech by the quiet Barbara surprised everyone.

'I know what you mean, Barbie,' said Janet. 'Let's forgive Susie – and let her help if she wants to.'

But the boys drew the line at that. No – they didn't want Susie's help. Secretly they felt that she might be a bit too clever for them!

'Well – to come back to the point,' said Peter, 'we'll say that we believe what Susie said about seeing a light in the castle – and that means that the woman artist she saw wasn't telling the truth when she said she didn't stay there at night – and it does seem to mean, too, that the light must have been a signal! All right – to whom was she signalling – and why?'

'I think we boys ought to go up to the castle tonight and have another snoop round,' said Colin. 'I feel ashamed now that we ran away as we did! I'd feel better about it if we went up again, and tried to find out what really is going on.'

The other boys nodded. They felt the same. 'But no girls,' said Peter, firmly, seeing that Janet was about to speak. 'NO GIRLS.'

'There's *one* thing we haven't tried to solve,' said George. 'And that is – who on earth stole the telescope! The ordinary thief wouldn't want a thing like that – difficult to sell, and no real use to him! I should have thought he'd have taken the rug off the floor, or our lamp – something like that.'

'Yes, you're right,' said Peter. Then they all jumped as Jack slapped his knee and gave a cry. 'Listen! I bet I know who stole our telescope! *Whoever is hiding in the castle took it!* Susie told that woman artist about the telescope, and how we could see the castle with it, and even saw someone at the window – and if there is any funny business going on up there, that woman would know that our telescope would show it to any of us down here – if we happened to look through it at an awkward moment for them!'

'So someone popped down here last night, found the shed-door unlocked, went in and stole the telescope so that we couldn't spy on them!' finished Peter. 'Too easy for words! Bother Susie! If only she'd locked the shed, I bet they wouldn't have got in.'

'The thing is – what sort of funny business could be going on, up in the old castle?' wondered Janet. They all frowned and thought hard.

'It would make a really good hiding-place for anything stolen,' suggested Pam. 'Those dungeons would be fine for that.'

'But Susie said there was nothing there but pictures without frames,' said Colin. 'I suppose that woman had painted them, and was storing them there till she could get them framed.'

'Don't be an idiot,' said Jack. 'If there were

376

a lot there, it would have taken anyone *weeks* to paint them. But I tell you what they *might* be! *Old* pictures – valuable ones!'

'Well, they would be framed, if so,' said Barbara.

'Not if they were stolen,' said Jack. 'Nothing easier than to take pictures out of their frames, roll them up, and spirit them away!'

'I think that's rather far-fetched,' objected Janet. 'Honestly I do.'

'All right,' said Jack. 'There's only one thing to do, as far as I can see – and that's to go up there tonight, and watch. Susie said that woman must have been signalling with a light last night. Right – she was presumably signalling to *someone* – probably telling them that the goods were there – they could come and fetch them – or something like that. In which case . . .'

'*Somebody* might go for them tonight!' said George and Jack together.

There was a silence, and everyone thought hard. Then Peter spoke firmly.

'This is what I think our plan should be. We four boys will bike up there again after supper tonight. We will snoop round and see what we can find out. I bet our telescope's hidden up there! If we think we need help, or that Dad ought to know and get busy too, we'll signal with one of our bike lamps. Wave it up and down!'

'Oooh – this is exciting!' said Pam. 'How many times will you wave?'

'Twice if everything's OK, and we can't find anything wrong. Four times if we'd like Dad to come up. More than four times if it's really *urgent*. Got that?'

'Yes,' said everyone, fervently, their eyes shining with excitement.

'Pam and Barbara, you come round after supper and watch with me,' said Janet. 'But wait a minute, Peter – how can we see your signals? We haven't the telescope now, remember, and we can't see any signals without that. The castle is too far away.'

'I've thought of that,' said Peter. 'You must borrow Dad's field-glasses – and I think, when we've been gone about half an hour, you'd better tell him the whole story, so that he's ready to come if we need him.'

'This is too exciting for words!' said Pam.

'Field-glasses! How clever you are, Peter. Of course, field-glasses can see nearly as far as a telescope – they will pick up any signal easily.'

'The meeting is ended,' said Peter, and Scamper got up with a sigh of relief and stretched himself. What a dull meeting – no buns, no biscuits, just talk, talk, talk – and hardly a laugh, and not one single pat! No – Scamper didn't at all approve of meetings like that! He stalked up the path with his tail down.

'Ooooh – twice if it's OK – four times if they want Peter's father to come – and six times if it's urgent!' said Barbara to Pam, as they went home. 'Pam – don't you think that the Secret Seven have a *thrilling* time?'

CHAPTER SIXTEEN

After supper

AFTER SUPPER that night, Peter disappeared to get his bicycle, and to meet the others. 'Now remember, Janet,' he said, as he went out. 'Borrow the field-glasses and use them – but you needn't ask Dad for them for a while – give us time to get well away, or Dad might come after us, and if there's nothing going on up there, it would be a shame to drag him out when he's tired; but be sure and WATCH FOR ANY SIGNAL.'

'Oh I will, Peter, I will,' said Janet, wishing she was going too. 'Oh, I do so want to come along too. Are you taking Scamper?'

'No. It's too far for him,' said Peter. 'Sorry, Scamper, old thing. Stay home!'

Scamper turned away sadly, tail down again, very miserable. Didn't Peter love him any more? This was the second time that he had gone out without him. Scamper walked down the garden some way behind Peter, wondering where he was going. He watched him take out his bicycle. He saw the other boys come up one by one, and his tail went down even further.

He could bear it no longer when he saw the boys ride off. He would follow them! They would go faster than he could run, but somehow he would smell their trail and follow. 'Wuff,' said Scamper to himself. 'Peter won't know. But I feel as if I MUST be with him tonight!'

And so a lonely figure padded up the road

after the bicycles, holding its nose in the air, sniffing, sniffing, trotting away after the four boys. Good old Scamper!

Meantime Janet was watching the clock. She was glad when the two other girls came. Time was going very slowly indeed. She waited until the boys had been gone about half an hour, and then she decided to ask for the field-glasses, and tell her parents what was happening! Would they be cross? Well, it couldn't be helped, she must just bear it.

She found the field-glasses and went to the sitting-room where her father and mother sat, her mother knitting and her father doing his accounts.

'Dad,' she said. 'May I borrow your field-glasses, please?'

'What in the world for?' said her father, astonished. 'At this time of night too!'

And then out everything came – the whole story, higgledy-piggledy at first, so that her parents couldn't make head or tail of what she was telling them. But gradually they understood what had been happening – and why Janet wanted the field-glasses!

'Bless us all!' said her father, quite astounded. 'What on earth will you children be up to next? This is a silly business – cycling up to the castle in the dark! As if anything serious could be happening there! Peter's idea of stolen pictures is *nonsense*!'

'Wait a minute, dear,' said his wife. 'I read something in the paper about valuable old paintings being stolen from Lord Lunwood's house – they were cut from their frames – and must have been rolled up and taken away quite easily – in a suitcase, I think the paper said . . .'

Janet gave an excited little scream. 'Oh, *Mother* – the pictures Susie and Binkie saw were just rolled up, too – not framed – oh, MOTHER!'

And now her parents really did sit up and take notice. They questioned Janet quickly, and were most astonished at all she told them.

'So the four boys have gone up to the castle, all on their own!' said her father. 'This is really a most extraordinary story, Janet, I feel rather worried.'

'You needn't be,' said Janet. 'The boys can look after themselves, Dad – they always have! We can watch for their signal, and see if they need help.'

'I'm not waiting for any signal!' said her father, firmly. 'I'm going up now – and I'm taking Matt the shepherd with me, and the gardener as well!'

'Oh dear!' said Janet. 'We were supposed to wait for a signal. Peter *will* be cross!'

'Well, I shan't mind *that*!' said her father, and went out to get Matt and to tell him to fetch the gardener. They were all to go up in the car.

Janet held the glasses carefully. Then she

suddenly remembered that she hadn't seen Scamper for some time. 'Wherever is he?' she thought. 'Poor old Scamper! I expect he's sulking in a corner somewhere, because the boys went off without him. I must find him and comfort him!'

She went back to where Pam and Barbara were patiently waiting in the playroom for her, and told them quickly what her father was going to do. They whole-heartedly approved.

'Grown-ups always seem to know *at once* what's the best thing to do,' said Pam, thankfully. 'That's one of the differences between them and us! Where are you off to now, Janet?'

'To look for old Scamper,' said Janet. 'Come with me.'

But, of course, they couldn't find Scamper. He was nowhere about, and Janet suddenly felt sure he had gone trailing after the boys. She was very glad.

'Scamper's always a help, anyway,' she said to the others. 'Come on – we'd better go up to the boxroom now and watch for signals through the field-glasses. Oh dear – I feel all worked up!'

But though they looked and looked through the glasses, each taking a turn, no signal came!

'This is awful,' said Janet, when an hour had gone by. 'No "All's Well" signal – and no "Something's Wrong" signal – and no "Urgent" signal – nothing at all! Whatever CAN be happening?'

CHAPTER SEVENTEEN

Up in the castle

QUITE A lot had been happening! The boys had set off on their bicycles, all feeling excited. They didn't know that Scamper was padding a long way behind them, sniffing most exciting night-smells as he went. He smelt a hedgehog somewhere in the ditch nearby, but paid no attention. Then he smelt rabbits in the field, and he longed to scatter them. But on he trotted! He was determined to find Peter and see what he was up to. It wasn't fair of Peter to leave him behind!

Peter was now almost at the castle, with the others cycling behind him up the steep hill. How they panted – but as long as *Peter* was still valiantly pedalling, they meant to as well! They were very thankful to see him jump off when he came to the place in the hedge where they had all flung their bicycles before! It had been a hard climb.

'Switch off your lamps,' said Peter. 'I think it will be safe to leave the bikes here. Only the bus comes by usually at night – very few cars.'

They were soon walking cautiously up the grassy hill towards the castle, which loomed above them like a gigantic black shadow. Each of them had a torch, but nobody used one, for fear of warning anybody in the castle. Peter suddenly stopped, not far from the old ruin.

'Go cautiously now,' he commanded. 'In single file – and remember, if trouble comes, one of us must signal with his torch. It doesn't matter which of us – so watch out in case it's necessary.'

They came quietly to the castle. Not a sound was to be heard. It was in complete darkness. When they stepped cautiously inside, their rubber shoes making no sound, a rustling noise began above their heads, and they stopped in fright.

'It's only the roosting jackdaws!' whispered

Peter. 'They must have heard our quiet tread! Wait till they settle again.'

Soon there was complete quiet once more. The boys went on down the great hall – and then Peter caught sight of something that made his heart beat quickly.

'Look – there's a light of some sort in that old kitchen-room,' he whispered to the others. 'Stay here. I'm going to see what it is.'

He tiptoed off to the entrance of the huge old room – and stopped in surprise at what he saw. Someone was there – a woman. She had lit a fire of sticks to keep her warm, and it was burning brightly. She was lying on her side, facing the little fire, her eyes closed.

'So it was *she* who had stamped out that half-burnt fire we found the other day, the twigs still warm!' thought Peter. 'She must have seen us coming, and hurriedly put it out. I hope she's really *sound* asleep!'

She seemed to be. She was lying on a mattress, wrapped all round in rugs (the ones Susie saw down in the dungeons, thought Peter) and didn't move at all. Beside her Peter caught a gleam of a clock's luminous

hands, and then his ears picked up its quick ticking.

He tiptoed away and whispered what he had seen to the others. 'She's fast asleep by a fire of twigs. I expect she's here to watch out for anyone coming in the daytime who might discover the secrets of the dungeon. It was really quite a good idea to pretend to be an artist and paint the castle – she could sit all day and keep guard, then!'

'Well, she didn't spot *us* the other day!' said Jack. 'Hey – if she's asleep, I don't think much

can be happening tonight, do you? I mean –
wouldn't she be awake if somebody was coming
in answer to her signal last night?'

'Yes. I suppose she would,' said Peter. 'Oh
well – we can at least go down to the dungeons
and see if those pictures are there! If they are,
we could pick them up and go home with them
– then the thieves would have a real shock when
they came – they'd find them gone!'

'Good idea!' said George, pleased. 'Let's go
down now – but for pity's sake don't let's wake
that sleeping woman! Go carefully.'

So, very warily indeed, the four boys went
down the old stone dungeon steps. These were
much broken and worn, and the boys were glad
of their torches to see where they were treading.

'Here we are!' said Peter, when they came at
last to the bottom of the steps. 'Whew – what
an *awful* place!'

It certainly was! It had great stone walls,
black with the dirt of centuries, and the floor
was of uneven stone too. Peter shone his torch
round and saw great iron staples in the wall.

'I bet plenty of poor wretched prisoners were
once roped to those for months – perhaps

years,' he said, and everyone shivered at the thought.

'It's not *damp* here, though,' said Jack. 'I thought all dungeons were damp and smelly.'

'Well, this is on a hill, so any water would drain away,' said Peter. 'And, of course, that's why this is a good hiding-place for valuable pictures – it's perfectly dry! Damp would have ruined them at once.'

'Well – where *are* the rolled-up canvases that Susie told us about?' said Jack, flashing his torch all round. 'There's straw here – where maybe tramps rest at times – and some old newspapers – but I can't see much else!'

Jack was right. There were no rolled-up pictures to be found, though they searched everywhere in the great old dungeons.

'Well – I suppose the men have been here already and taken them,' said George, in disappointment.

'Or else Susie made it up!' said Colin. 'Another of her little tricks!'

'No,' said Jack. 'I am certain she didn't make that up. Binkie saw the canvases too, you know. And yet – if the thieves *have* been to fetch them, why is that woman still here? It must surely mean that she has hidden them somewhere else – maybe because she was afraid that the girls had seen the pictures, and might tell someone.'

'Yes. That's more like it,' said Peter. 'But where can they be hidden? They must be somewhere easy to get at, if the men are coming here for them. They wouldn't want to spend ages getting them out of some difficult hiding-place!'

'Well – there's nothing for it but to do a bit of hunting ourselves!' said Colin. 'Come on! And let's hope we find our telescope somewhere too!'

CHAPTER EIGHTEEN

An exciting discovery

So, TREADING very quietly indeed, not daring even to cough, the boys began to look for a likely hiding-place. They hunted in every corner, except in the room where the woman lay asleep, and at last came to the conclusion that the pictures must be somewhere there. It seemed to be the only place left!

'She's probably hidden them under her mattress,' said Peter, with a small groan. 'But let's have one last think. Where would *we* hide them if we had to? And remember, they *could* be straightened out flat.'

Silence. Everyone thought hard. Then Colin whispered loudly: 'I know where *I'd* hide them

– under all the mess of twigs the jackdaws have dropped for years, at the base of the big tower!'

'Good idea!' whispered back Peter. 'Fine hiding-place! We'll go and look. Quietly now!' he admonished, as a scramble started.

They tiptoed to where the mass of twigs lay heaped everywhere on the floor, and shone their torches all around. 'It looks as if that pile over there has been messed about a bit,' whispered George, shining his torch on a heaped stack. 'Hold my torch. I'll scrabble about and see.'

He stepped over the masses of twigs, and they cracked loudly beneath his feet. He stopped in a hurry, and waited a moment, afraid that the noise would wake the sleeping woman. Then he leaned forward and began carefully to scrape away the twigs that seemed to have been freshly heaped-up.

His hand felt something underneath, and he gave a small cry. 'I believe I've found something!' he whispered, and pulled out what looked rather like a roll of thick paper.

'Yes! It's one of the pictures Susie must have

seen down in the dungeons!' said Peter, thrilled. 'See if there are any more.'

Yes – there were plenty more, all neatly rolled up, some of them inside one another. George handed them all out to Peter and Jack. It was a very thrilling moment indeed!

And then they heard something that startled them very much, and made them jump almost out of their skins! A bell! A loud bell that rang and rang and rang, breaking the dark silence so suddenly that the boys felt rooted to the spot. Then the noise stopped, and there was silence again.

'What was it? A telephone bell ringing?' whispered Colin.

'Sounded more like an alarm clock going off,' whispered George, surprised to find himself trembling.

'Of course! It was the clock we heard ticking near that sleeping woman!' said Peter. 'She had set it for a certain time! Maybe the thieves are coming soon, to get the hidden pictures, and she wanted to be sure to be awake. We'd better hide!'

They tiptoed to a small recess in the great wall, and crouched there, their hearts beating fast. Peter and Jack had the rolled-up pictures. They waited there, quite silent.

They heard movements after a minute or two, and then the light of a lamp came from the kitchen-like room where the woman had been sleeping. The light came nearer, and the crouching boys saw the woman pass their recess, holding the light before her to see the way. They huddled in the dark shadows, hardly daring to breathe!

She passed right by, went to the great entrance, and stood there. 'She's signalling!' whispered

Peter. 'I bet that's to say "All's Clear – come and get the goods"!'

'Oh goodness! The girls at home will see the signal and think it's *ours*!' groaned Jack. 'I wonder how many times that woman's waving.'

'Let's get out of here,' said Colin. 'I don't want to be found by whoever's coming up to the castle. Let's go now, whilst we've time.'

'Well, we should have plenty of time, if the thieves have to come from any distance,' said Peter. 'But maybe they're hiding somewhere near, so we'll have to look out! Come on – we'll

rush by that woman – she *will* have a fright! Let's hope we can signal with our torches when we get out on the hillside!'

They all left the dark little recess and raced to the entrance, where the woman stood, the lamp still in her hand. She gave a scream when they pushed past her, and tried to catch hold of Colin.

'Stop! Who are you? Stop, I say!'

But the boys did not stop. They tore out into the darkness. Then Peter had a shock – he tripped over something and fell headlong – and down went all the others too! Before they could get up, firm hands had hold of them, and each

boy was pulled roughly to his feet. A bright torch was shone into their faces.

'Kids!' said a man's voice. 'Four boys! What on earth are you doing here, I'd like to know!'

Three men stood there, dark shadows in the night, lit only by the torch they held towards the four boys. They had neatly tripped each of them as they came racing out into the darkness.

'Let me go!' yelled Peter, and kicked out hard. The man holding him tightened his grip.

'Quite a little spitfire,' he said, mockingly, and shook him hard. The woman came up, then, amazed.

'I've not seen them before,' she said. 'They must have been hiding in the castle.'

'Are the things safe?' said the tallest man, sharply.

'I'll see,' she said, and went off. The boys waited, their hearts thumping. They knew that the pictures were certainly *not* safe in their hiding-place. No – they were well down the hillside now, where they had rolled after Peter and Jack had kicked them, as soon as the men caught hold of their arms. How they hoped that nobody had seen the rolls of pictures bumping down the hillside in the darkness!

The woman came hurrying back. 'They're gone!' she said. 'Not a single one there. These boys must have taken them and hidden them somewhere! Whatever made them come here? They *couldn't* have known anything about them!'

'We'll soon find out,' said the tall man. 'Shove the boys into the dungeons and keep them there till they tell us what they are doing here at this time of night – and where they've put the pictures!'

And then, very roughly indeed, the four boys were pushed into the castle, and down into the dungeons! What a horrible thing to happen, just as they had been about to go home in triumph!

CHAPTER NINETEEN

A friend in need!

'OH NO! This is a sickening thing to happen!' said Peter, rubbing himself where he had fallen against the hard stone floor. 'What bad luck to run headlong into those men!'

'Peter! What happened to the pictures?' said George, in a whisper.

'We managed to drop them and give them a good kick down the hill,' answered Peter. 'I hope they're still rolling!'

'What are we going to do?' asked Colin, who felt decidedly scared.

'I don't see that we can do *anything* at the moment,' said Peter. 'What a pity we weren't able to signal to the girls, after all! Then we'd know help was coming.'

'What do you suppose those men are doing?' asked George. 'Looking for the pictures?'

'I should think so,' said Peter. 'They'll be down here soon enough, when they can't find them anywhere!'

Nobody liked hearing that! Their hearts sank. Peter began to wonder if he could possibly get out of the castle and signal home. No. He couldn't. One of the men would be sure to be watching at the top of the dungeon steps.

And then something most astonishing happened! There was no *man* at the top of the steps – only the woman, who had been told to shout if the boys tried to escape. Quite suddenly the boys heard her give a scream, and then she shouted, 'Oh, what is it, what is it?'

Then something bounded down the steps at top speed, and flung itself on top of Peter, whining in delight!

'*Scamper!*' cried Peter, in the utmost astonishment. 'Whatever are *you* doing here? How did you find us? Oh good dog, clever dog! Oh, how glad I am to see you!'

Scamper whined and barked and licked every one of the boys. What a long, long trek he had had, following their trail – but now, here he was, *just* at the right moment! He leapt up at Peter, and went almost mad with joy.

The boys felt braver at once. Scamper would be a real help! The woman's screams had brought the men up at once, and they shouted to her.

'What's happening? What is it?'

'Oh, something pushed by me in the dark and shot down into the dungeon!' she said. 'It *seemed* to be a *dog*!'

Scamper immediately produced an extremely fierce growl down at the bottom of his throat – it startled even Peter, who was used to Scamper's barks and growls.

'Urrrrr. URRRRRR, URRRRRRRR!'

'You be careful of our dog!' yelled Peter. 'He'll attack you if you don't let us go.'

'You tell us where you've put those pictures and we'll let you go all right,' came back the angry answer. 'Otherwise we'll keep you here for a week!'

'Rubbish!' shouted back Peter. 'Our people will soon come after us. *We* don't mind staying here. Makes a nice change!'

All the same, the boys didn't at all like being down in the dungeons. They were dark and full of shadows – and they were very cold indeed! One of the men decided to give the boys a scare and came rushing down the steps, hallooing at the top of his voice. He certainly startled the boys – but as he also had the effect of making Scamper go wild with rage, it didn't do him much good! The spaniel flew at him, and nipped him smartly on the leg. The man gave a howl and went up the steps as quickly as he had come down!

'Good dog, Scamper,' said Peter, pleased. 'Gosh, I'm glad you trailed us tonight! What a long walk you've had, old fellow! You're a really good friend!'

For about an hour nothing happened. What were the men doing? Having a meal? Looking for the pictures? Nobody could guess. They all felt very thankful that Scamper was there to protect them.

'We wouldn't have had a chance without him!' said Peter. Then he stiffened as he heard a distant noise. 'Listen – something's going on! Listen to that shouting and yelling!'

They listened – and Scamper suddenly gave a delighted whine and tore up the stone steps at top speed.

'Hey, come back!' yelled Peter – but Scamper took no notice.

'Let's go and see what's happening,' said Peter, and started up the steps. 'There can't be anyone guarding us now, if Scamper shot away like that.'

They all went cautiously up the steps – and, as Peter said, there was no one on guard at the top. But outside the castle there was certainly *something* going on! Shouts and yells and the sound of feet stamping about – what a to-do! Scamper was in the midst of it, barking and nipping whenever he had a chance! Quick, Peter – where's your torch?

CHAPTER TWENTY

Safe home again!

PETER SHONE his torch on to the shouting mob
– and nearly dropped it in surprise. 'DAD! How
did *you* get here! And *Matt*! Hey, look – there's
Dad and Matt and the gardener – and they've
caught all three of the men!'

The torches shone on the six men and the

excited dog. There was no sign of the woman – she had fled away while she had the chance!

'Now then – you just come along quietly,' said Matt's deep voice. The big shepherd was having the time of his life! He could handle bulls and cows and horses and rams and goodness knows what – and he had no difficulty at all in handling two or three frightened men, especially with Peter's father and the hefty gardener to help.

'Dad! Oh, Dad! How did you know we wanted help – we weren't able to signal!' cried Peter, as his father neatly pinioned his man's arms behind him.

'Hallo, Peter – so you're all right!' said his father. 'We're just taking these men down to their van to lock them in and Matt will drive them down to the police-station. I'm sure the police will give them a bed tonight! We found their van parked up the lane, ready to take them off again – with the pictures too, I suppose! We saw your bikes somewhere down the lane as well!'

'Oh, *Dad*! I can't believe you're here!' said Peter, full of thankfulness. 'I suppose Janet told you where we were. Can we do anything to help you with these men?'

'No – but you might look around for those pictures,' said his father. 'They're too valuable to be left in the damp and cold. These fellows won't tell us where they are.'

'Perhaps that woman took them,' suggested Matt, marching the tall man away in front of him. 'She scuttled off like a rabbit.'

'No – she didn't take them,' said Peter. '*I* know where they are! I'll get them!'

He and the others raced down the hill with their torches to find where the rolled-up pictures had gone. Now – where were they? Surely that woman hadn't found them? No – there they were, lying where they had rolled, safe and sound, spread all about the hillside!

'Good!' said Peter, and pounced on them. Soon he and the boys had gathered them all, and ran back to where the men were now being bundled into their own van. They stared angrily when they saw the rolls of canvases carried by the boys.

Matt drove away in the van, with the three angry, frightened men locked inside. Peter's father and the gardener went to the car in which they had driven up.

'You boys will come down on your bikes, won't you?' Peter's father shouted. 'What about Scamper?'

'Oh take him in the car, Dad, if you will,' said Peter, lifting up the excited dog. 'He walked all the way here, dear old fellow – he must be tired now!'

Scamper was thankful to go back in the car. Peter's father carefully put the precious canvases out of his reach, and away they went down the hill, following the van.

What a joyful meeting the Seven had in Peter's playroom, as soon as they arrived back. The girls and Peter's mother gave them a great welcome and could hardly wait to hear their news – and how eagerly they listened to the four boys' exciting story.

'Oh, *what* a time you had!' said Janet, her eyes shining. 'Oh, I *wish* I'd been with you! Whatever will Susie and Binkie say when they hear all this? By the way, did you find our telescope in the castle? I suppose the men had hidden it somewhere there?'

'No – we didn't find the telescope!' said Jack. 'Bother! We ought to have asked those men where it was – our marvellous telescope that brought us this exciting adventure!'

'Here's Dad back again,' said Peter, hearing the front door open, and Scamper's loud barking as he too came in, and rushed up the stairs. Peter opened the playroom door, and Scamper jumped up at him in joy.

'Dad! We're all up here, Mother too!' called Peter. 'Oh, Dad – THANK you for coming to our rescue! We couldn't even give the signal for help – so we'd all be down in those miserable dungeons still, if you hadn't rescued us. Oh, Dad – wasn't it exciting!'

'Excuse me,' said Jack, anxiously, 'did the

men say anything about my telescope? We're pretty sure they stole it because they knew we were watching the castle through it.'

'Oh yes – they've admitted that they stole it,' said Peter's father. 'But I'm sorry to have to tell you that they didn't take it up to the castle – they simply threw it away into the river.'

'Oh my goodness!' said Jack, looking very down in the dumps. 'That's a blow. It was such a *wonderful* telescope – I'll never, never have another like it.'

'You will, old chap!' said Peter's father. 'There's a reward offered for those pictures – a pretty good one too – and as it will go to the Secret Seven of course, I'm sure that at their next meeting they will agree to buying you a *magnificent* telescope, Jack – and there will be enough money over for the Seven to save for a very good Christmas, as well – you certainly deserve it!'

'And Scamper, you shall have the *biggest* bone we can buy you!' said Janet, patting the spaniel's silky head. 'Oh I'm longing for our next Secret Seven meeting – we'll have such plans to make!'

You will, Janet! How we'd like to listen in and hear your excited voices, planning how to spend that reward – a fine new telescope for Jack and Susie – a bone for Scamper – a lovely Christmas for everyone. And I'm sure we can all guess what your *next* password will be – PICTURES! Are we right, Peter?

THE
SECRET
SEVEN

Solve the mystery!

If you can't wait to solve another mystery,
read the next book in the series

Shock For The Secret Seven

The Famous Five
Join the adventure!

Enid Blyton

is one of the most popular children's authors of all time. Her books have sold over 500 million copies and have been translated into other languages more often than any other children's author.

Enid Blyton adored writing for children. She wrote over 600 books and hundreds of short stories. *The Famous Five* books, now 75 years old, are her most popular. She is also the author of other favourites including *The Secret Seven*, *The Magic Faraway Tree*, *Malory Towers* and *Noddy*.

Born in London in 1897, Enid lived much of her life in Buckinghamshire and adored dogs, gardening and the countryside. She was very knowledgeable about trees, flowers, birds and animals. Dorset – where some of the Famous Five's adventures are set – was a favourite place of hers too.

Enid Blyton's stories are read and loved by millions of children (and grown-ups) all over the world. Visit enidblyton.com to discover more.